AUG — 2018

YA Fic DOKTORSKI
Doktorski, Jennifer Salvato,
August and everything after /
33341008014614

P9-DVP-828

"A thoug_____tance of learning to adapt to changes large and small."

—*Kirkus Reviews*

"Doktorski has crafted a rich, multilayered novel with a strong sense of place and a good mix of characters and problems."

—*Booklist*

"Doktorski has created a multidimensional character in Lucy and placed her in a fully developed novel."

—*VOYA*

"[A] marvelous novel… Highly recommend it to romance lovers everywhere."

—*TeenReads.com*

Also by Jennifer Salvato Doktorski

The Summer After You and Me

WITHDRAWN

AUGUST AND
EVERYTHING AFTER

WITHDRAWN

August and Everything After

JENNIFER SALVATO DOKTORSKI

Alameda Free Library
1550 Oak Street
Alameda, CA 94501

sourcebooks
fire

Copyright © 2018 by Jennifer Salvato Doktorski
Cover and internal design © 2018 by Sourcebooks, Inc.
Cover design by Vanessa Han
Cover images © Michela Ravasio/Stocksy; Rachel Juliet Lerch/Shutterstock

Sourcebooks and the colophon are registered trademarks of Sourcebooks, Inc.

All rights reserved. No part of this book may be reproduced in any form or by
any electronic or mechanical means including information storage and retrieval
systems—except in the case of brief quotations embodied in critical articles or
reviews—without permission in writing from its publisher, Sourcebooks, Inc.

The characters and events portrayed in this book are fictitious or are used ficti-
tiously. Any similarity to real persons, living or dead, is purely coincidental and
not intended by the author.

All brand names and product names used in this book are trademarks, registered
trademarks, or trade names of their respective holders. Sourcebooks, Inc., is not
associated with any product or vendor in this book.

Published by Sourcebooks Fire, an imprint of Sourcebooks, Inc.
P.O. Box 4410, Naperville, Illinois 60567-4410
(630) 961-3900
Fax: (630) 961-2168
sourcebooks.com

Library of Congress Cataloging-in-Publication Data

Names: Doktorski, Jennifer Salvato, author.
Title: August and everything after / Jennifer Salvato Doktorski.
Description: Naperville, Illinois : Sourcebooks Fire, [2018] | Summary:
    "Summer on the New Jersey shore offers Quinn a new start at life and love,
    but only if she can come to terms with her past"-- Provided by publisher.
Identifiers: LCCN 2017051905 | (pbk. : alk. paper)
Subjects: | CYAC: Conduct of life--Fiction. | Dating (Social
    customs)--Fiction. | Musicians--Fiction. | Mothers and daughters--Fiction.
    | Family life--New Jersey--Fiction. | New Jersey--Fiction.
Classification: LCC PZ7.D69744 Aug 2018 | DDC [Fic]--dc23 LC record avail-
able at https://lccn.loc.gov/2017051905

Printed and bound in the United States of America.
VP 10 9 8 7 6 5 4 3 2 1

For my amazing niece and nephew,
Cassie Grace and Anthony James Collucci,
with love.

ONE

I started wearing my grandmother's old cat-eye glasses in June, right after my latest crush nearly crushed me. The messy incident involved my band student teacher, a six-pack of Blue Moon, and a freak thunderstorm. Connect the dots any way you want. I know it's not pretty. Neither was I when I put on Grammy's glasses. But that was kind of the point. When I fled my small town after graduation to spend the summer at my aunt's beach house, I didn't want to be the old Quinn Gallo anymore. Here at the Jersey shore, no one knows me as the half-naked girl who had to be rescued from her band teacher's Toyota Corolla by the Jaws of Life.

The glasses added a layer to my new anonymity. I found them tucked in the top drawer of the wicker dresser as I unpacked in the guest room, and something inside me shifted when I put on the black, bejeweled frames. Like the first time Bilbo slipped on the One Ring of Power.

I got the prescription adjusted to fit me and I've been wearing them ever since.

In fact, I'm wearing them tonight as I sit on a barstool at Keegan's Cocktail Lounge, the old-man bar turned indie rock club where I waitress on Friday nights. I'm reading *The Awakening* while the opening act—a singer/songwriter dude with a backstory more tragic than my own—sets up. It's his first performance since his guitarist and drummer were killed in a tour bus accident two years ago. My coworker, Liam, told me all about it.

"Malcolm was really messed up. He blamed himself." I told Liam I couldn't imagine, but unfortunately, I could. My best friend, Lynn, died when we were fifteen.

So I've been avoiding Malcolm since he got here, knowing that if I'm not careful, I'll get pulled into his orbit. Fuckups attract fuckups, I'm sure of it.

Apparently I'm ignoring him better than I thought, because he manages to sneak up behind me, lean down so that we're almost cheek to cheek, and peek through my glasses. I startle and face him.

"What the hell are you doing?" I ask, louder than I intended.

"Sorry," he says. "I had to know if those glasses were real or some hipster gimmick."

Before I can stop myself, I reach up and tug his beard. "I was thinking the same thing about this."

"Ouch. I usually get a girl's name before she grabs my facial hair. Or anything else."

He wishes.

I put down my book and hold out my hand.

"Quinn Gallo."

He holds my gaze and hand longer than he needs to, swinging my arm a little like we're about to twirl a jump rope.

"Malcolm Trent."

I pull away.

"I know." I flick my thumb toward the flyer taped to the mirror behind the bar. "I can read."

He nods toward my book.

"I see. Is that the feminist lit talking or are you always like this?"

I twist the leather cuff bracelet I never take off and think of something nice to say. It's not his fault he's immune to Grammy's glasses. "I'm looking forward to your set."

"Yeah? But you brought backup entertainment just in case?"

"Reading is work, not entertainment. My aunt's letting me live with her this summer on the condition that I read one book a week. Her picks."

"What else have you read?"

I tick off my reading list thus far.

"*Jane Eyre*, *Beloved*, *The Bell Jar*—"

"It's possible your aunt needs to lighten up."

I shrug.

"Small price to pay for a summer away from home. I had to get away from my town."

"Trouble with the law?"

"More like trouble with The Mom. I'm not her favorite daughter at the moment."

My "poor judgment" regarding my unromantic evening with my band teacher coupled with my decision not to go to college this fall landed Mom and I on opposite sides of an enormous iceberg. We both needed time to thaw.

"Ha! I could write a book about being the prodigal son."

"Can you make it a song instead? If you write a book, my aunt will make me read it."

Malcolm's reflexive laugh warms my body. He looks like he's about to say something else, but before he has a chance, Caleb, the owner of Keegan's, signals Malcolm that it's time to take the stage.

"I gotta—"

"Oh, yeah, of course. I've gotta get to work too."

Neither of us moves.

I stare at him over the top of my glasses. He tilts his head like he's deciding what to do next. Then, before I have time to register what's happening, Malcolm reaches toward my face and gently pushes my glasses back up my nose.

"You have pretty eyes, Quinn. You shouldn't hide them behind ugly glasses."

For the first time in my life, someone looked me in the eyes and didn't point out that they're two different colors. The right one is brown, the left is blue. I want to say thank you, or have a good set, or *something*, but by the time I get my voice back, he's gone.

I smooth my apron, pick up my book, and try to shake off the feeling that my defensive shield just failed me and allowed my next nobody to walk right through.

TWO

Nobodies. That's what my younger, wiser sister, Evie, calls the guys I attract and/or obsess over.

It's hard to argue with her. I've had a bad run.

Sophomore year I unceremoniously lost my virginity to Sammy the Snake. The nickname alone should have tipped me off that a sexting scandal with some girl named Brittany was in his future, but my best friend had recently died and I wasn't thinking. Junior year I had a thing for the Austrian exchange student, Ralph. We had a friends-with-benefits arrangement for most of the school year before he blew me off. Brokenhearted, I retreated to my bedroom to listen to sad songs and study Jeff Buckley lyrics until Ralph boarded his jet back to Vienna.

Halfway through my senior year, Mr. G—a guy with one

tie and a limited number of dress pants—walked into the band room and took up residence in my geek love fantasies. I thought I caught him staring at me a few times as I lugged my drum to the storage room, but figured I'd imagined it. Up until then, all my romantic relationships had been exactly that: imagined. Or maybe unrequited? Same thing, I guess. The good parts were all in my head. Then on the last day of band, two days before graduation, he left a note on my snare: *Need to talk to you about something, and it has nothing to do with band.*

After Lynn died, I had some definite ideas about what I did and didn't deserve. I'd skipped homecoming dances, parties, college visits, talent show tryouts, and student council fund-raisers. I was one of only six senior girls who didn't get asked to prom. When I got that note, I thought my cosmic debt had been repaid, that it was okay to want to really connect with someone again. I took it as a sign from the universe.

After my one and only "date" with Mr. G made the local news, I figured the universe was telling me we weren't quite even-stevens yet.

"You can't keep giving the best parts of yourself away to some nobody," Evie had said after the oak branch and my reputation came crashing down.

I'm so caught up flipping through my mental scrapbook of Love Gone Wrong that I bump into Liam as he's washing glasses behind the bar in Keegan's. He's wearing his "uniform"—a black tee that says "Barback. I can't pour beer. Please stop asking." Barbacks are like busboys for the bartenders. They clean up and stock shelves but don't serve.

"Sorry," I say.

Liam says nothing. Just smirks.

"What?" He's making me paranoid.

"Nothin'."

Yeah, right. I know Liam, and that face is not nothing. I start filling the crystal-like bowls we keep on the bar with trail mix, because Keegan's is fancy like that, and pretend I don't care what Liam has to say. I can wait.

"Saw you talking to Malcolm," he says.

Here we go. "And?"

"Looked like you two were having a moment."

"A moment? There was no moment. I told him I was looking forward to his set. He told me my glasses were ugly."

Liam laughs.

"You know, Q, it wouldn't kill you to get a new pair…and a new wardrobe."

Rude. I love the vintage Doc Martens and sleeveless plaid shirt I'm wearing. Both belonged to my aunt Annie, a diehard Gen Xer who's convinced the music world is ripe for a grunge revival.

"Where's Kiki tonight?" I ask. "I like you better when she's around."

I thought Liam was a douchebag when I first met him back

in June. Before he called me "Q" he called me "Benny," which is Jersey shore-speak for unwelcomed tourist. So there's that. But there's also the way he makes these big proclamations about music, picking apart every band that comes through here like *he* invented the three-chord pop song. He's grown on me in the past few weeks, in a poor-misunderstood-douchebag kind of way. His twin sister Lucy and friends are nice though, and Kiki, his girlfriend, is totally adorable. She keeps telling me we need to hang out.

"She'll be here soon," he says.

"Good. They invented the phrase *better half* for guys like you."

His wry smile tells me we get each other. Liam picks up a dishrag and snaps it in my direction, then proceeds to wipe down the bar.

"You know, Malcolm's looking to put a new band together. You play drums right?"

"I play drum, Liam. Drum."

"Oh, come on. I see you tapping out rhythms and working that fake kick drum with your foot when you watch the bands here."

My face heats up. He noticed me playing air drums?

"Liam, I do not—"

He puts up a hand.

"Bup bup bup. Don't try to deny it. My point is, snare is the hard part. It probably wouldn't take you long to learn to play a full kit."

I've been teaching myself to do that very thing (you could learn how to run your own island nation with YouTube), but I haven't told anyone.

"If he needs a drummer, he can find a better one than me."

Liam winks.

"But maybe not one he *likes* more than you."

I punch him in the arm. Kiddingly. Sort of.

"Ouch. I'm just saying. You should talk to Malcolm. We both should," Liam says.

Liam plays guitar, and from the way he talks about Malcolm and his legendary brush with fame, I know Liam would love to hitch his wagon to Malcolm's star, or whatever that saying is. But me playing drums in a rock band? *Pfff*. Yeah, right. I shake my head and snap out of it. Mom said I needed to come up with a solid life plan by the end of summer, not join a rock band.

"Liam!" Caleb calls out. "Watch the board."

Liam holds the dishrag in my direction.

"Can you please finish up for me?"

"All right. But only because you asked nicely." *Please* and *thank you* are the magic words.

Liam hustles toward the soundboard. In addition to barbacking, he took over sound duty from his friend Andrew Clark. Before I started here, Andrew quit Keegan's to be a counselor at a sleepaway camp. I hear about him *a lot*. How Andrew is the funniest person Liam knows. How Andrew once dated his sister. How Andrew was supposed to go to Rutgers with Liam, but decided to take a gap year until he decides what he wants to do. I know everything about this guy but his shoe size. Oh wait, I do know his shoe size. Nine and a half.

I get it. Liam misses his best friend. We have that in common, and it makes him seem like less of a know-it-all jerk.

I finish cleaning the bar and move out onto the floor to take drink orders from customers sitting in the booths. They each have faux portholes, remnants of Keegan's former life as a seafood restaurant.

Malcolm is all set up on the "stage" made of milk crates and wooden pallets. It's tucked in the corner under a ship wheel chandelier. I try not to let my eyes stray as I jot down orders, but my ears stay tuned to his frequency. Malcolm strums a few chords, then taps the mic and sings the line about a tired dream from The Replacements' "I'll Be You." I didn't know anyone under forty knew that song. Lucky for me, I'm my aunt's '90s alt-rock disciple. After the obligatory "check, one, two" into the vocal mic, he plays snippets of songs I've never heard before while Liam makes adjustments.

The standing room in front of the stage is filling up, mostly with underage kids. Kiki, Liam's sister Lucy, and Lucy's boyfriend Connor are among them. Big crowds are unusual for us. Keegan's is across the bay bridge from the barrier island, landlocked in a residential neighborhood without a tiki bar or water view. We appeal more to pale-skinned misanthropes and music snobs, who scorn sunny beaches and tourists in equal measure.

Guess Malcolm still has a lot of fans.

The excited chatter gets louder and the room hums with electricity like the air before a thunderstorm. My pulse kicks up a notch and my breath quickens. I don't know why, but I'm nervous for Malcolm.

Finally, Caleb steps up to the mic. He's got a few grays in his sideburns, and a slight paunch, but his cargo jeans, Converse high tops, and black tee camouflage his age well.

"It's been a while since he's been here," Caleb announces "But it's nice to have him back. Welcome, Malcolm Trent."

The brief intro is met with a round of ear-piercing whistles and applause. Malcolm doesn't wait for the noise to subside and just gets right to it, launching into a song everyone seems to know.

To be honest, he starts off a bit rough. Malcolm's voice is pitchy at times, his guitar playing not so smooth, but the crowd is behind him, singing along to every word. There's a sincerity about Malcolm, an earnestness, which makes him captivating to watch. I sneak peeks while scrambling to settle tabs at some tables and delivering hot wings and fresh rounds to others.

Malcolm's set gets better as he segues from one song to the next without stopping to banter with the audience or even make eye contact. It can't be easy for him, standing alone up there with the specter of his bandmates backing every song.

When his set's over, the crowd chants "one more song," and Malcolm finally looks out into the audience and blinks, like he's only now realized we're here.

"You guys want to hear a new one?"

The crowd responds with whoops and hollers, and Malcolm breaks into a grin so warm and genuine, I can almost see the little boy behind the beard and sad eyes.

"This one's called 'That Last Night,'" he says, and then fingerpicks the opening notes. When he strums the first chord and begins to sing, the lyrics could easily be mistaken for a breakup song, but I can tell it's an elegy.

That last night, that last time, that last look I can't erase/I should have said more, should have done more, found a way to take your place.

He's finally hit his stride and there's something about the combination of his voice—raspy and vulnerable—and the lyrics that trips a wire in my brain. *Not now, not now, not now,* I tell myself. But the flashes come so fast, I can't tamp them down. I see Lynn's face. A dark SUV. A helmet rolling toward the curb. My hands fumbling to dial 911. My skull tingles and my breath gets shallow. The mantras and phrases that usually help me keep these memories at bay aren't working. *I've got to get out of here.*

I plop my tray on the nearest table, twist my leather cuff bracelet, and scan the bar for the quickest escape route. I plunge into the crush of people. The next thing I know, I'm slamming open the front door and tumbling into the balmy July night.

Gasping, I reach into my pocket for the small, white pill wrapped in foil that I keep with me for emergencies and wait for the urge to swallow it to subside. I try not to take the Xanax unless I absolutely need it. Usually I can talk myself down. But tonight, the heavy air envelops me, making it hard to take deep breaths. Traffic swishes by; the warm breeze delivers the bay's briny scent. I press my back against the building, slide to the ground, count backward from one hundred, and wait.

"Hold your shit together, Quinn," I admonish myself, even though every nerve ending in my body is poised for a release. I don't have time for this. I need to get back inside. I unwrap the pill, snap it in half, and swallow it. I pinch the bridge of my nose, wait for it to work, and will myself not to cry. Because even though it doesn't happen often, once I start crying, I can't stop.

THREE

The door bangs open, jolting me back.

Malcolm steps outside, looking up at the sky, and lights a cigarette. He takes a deep inhale and does a double take when he sees me sitting there.

"Had to escape, huh? Was I that bad?"

I push myself to standing and dust off my butt.

"I wasn't escaping. You were great. That last song especially. The lyrics…the mood…it affected me."

He squints.

"Let me guess. Because you just broke up with your boyfriend?"

His slight condescension ignites anger inside me.

"Because my best friend died and it was my fault."

The force of my words causes him to flinch and me to take a step back. My heart beats so hard, the skin around my sternum pulses. I've never said that out loud to anyone. I'm not sure why I did now, except that I am Quinn Gallo, queen of the inappropriate and destroyer of casual conversation. If the cat-eye glasses didn't send him running, this will.

We lock eyes and I can't quite read his expression. My temple pulses, ticking off the seconds until I implode. And when I think I actually might shatter here in front of him, he drops his cigarette to the ground and crushes it with his heel. "Wait here. I'll be right back."

I lean back against the building, close my eyes, and let the calming effects of the Xanax wash over me. My breath slows and the tingling sensation abates.

"Quinn?" Malcolm's voice rouses me. "Are you okay?"

"I'm good."

I breathe in through my nose and open my eyes. Malcolm's holding a CD and a Sharpie. He pulls off the cap with his teeth and scrawls the word "Demos" and a phone number on the face of the disc.

"My new songs." The disc captures passing headlights on its mirrored surface as he holds it up and waves it so the marker dries. "Let me know what you think."

I'm not sure what I expected, but it wasn't this.

"I…thank you."

He opens the door and gestures for me to go in front of him.

"Don't thank me now. You haven't listened to them yet."

Back inside, he heads to the stage to pack up, and I hustle over to the bar to put the disc with my stuff before checking on my tables.

"Where the hell were you?" Liam asks when he sees me. "I was—"

He's about to get all whiny about how busy he was, but he spots the disc in my hand and makes that expression cats get when they see a shiny object.

"What's that?"

"Malcolm's new songs."

"Holy crap! I knew it. He likes you. You've got to get us an audition for his band."

"Stop it, Liam. He doesn't even know me. We barely spoke."

"Well, whatever you said, it left an impression."

Yeah, dead best friends will do that. But there's no way in hell I'm telling Liam what I said to Malcolm. That's kind of the whole point of me living here. To make my history *history*.

I shrug like it's no big deal.

"I told him I dug his new song. I'm sure everyone else will too."

I see Malcolm in my periphery, packing up his gear to make way for the next band. His progress is slowed by congratulatory handshakes and bro hugs.

Liam nods.

"He was good. He didn't kill it though. Malcolm's more of rhythm guitarist than a lead."

"Which is why he needs you?"

"Exactly," Liam grins.

I shake my head. "I gotta check my tables."

My customers are craning their necks to look for me as I walk across the bar—a clear signal I've been gone too long. Crap. I hope Caleb didn't notice. He's a friend of my aunt's and the reason I got a job here. I don't want to let him or my aunt down. Plus, I like it here in the land of misfit toys.

By the time I deliver fresh rounds to half my tables and clear glasses from the rest, Malcolm's by the door, looking ready to leave. I'm about to walk over there when I'm intercepted by Arnie, one of the regulars. He slips a five into my apron pocket.

I try to give back his money.

"Arnie, I didn't even serve you tonight."

Arnie shows up here stoned most nights and doesn't leave until he's also drunk. I figure something happened to Arnie—something he can't talk about and can't forget. Why else would he keep turning up here alone? Everyone calls him Elmo, on account of his striking red hair. But I always call him Arnie, and I think he appreciates it. That's why he tips me even when he doesn't have to.

His fingers curl around my hand and crumple the five-dollar bill.

"Keep it. Save it for your future."

Ha! My future.

"Thank you, but I'm more of a short-term kind of girl."

Right now, I can't see past August. What comes after that, who knows?

"Listen to me. You're a nice girl and the future will be here before you know it. One minute you're a kid with all these opportunities, and the next thing you know, you're forty-five like me and out of choices."

Holy crap—Arnie's only forty-five? I thought he was the same age as the Spoon Man. That's our other regular who's got to be at least sixty. He drinks boilermakers, talks about his Army days, and once he's had a few in him, plays the spoons.

"Okay then. Thanks, Arnie," I say, peering over his shoulder.

Normally I'd stay and chat with him longer, but we're busier than usual and I'm anxious to say goodbye to Malcolm. But by the time I sidestep Arnie, drop off my tray of empty glasses, and make my way toward the front door, Malcolm's already gone.

FOUR

For the rest of the night, I go through the motions of being a good waitress in a subpar bar, while counting down the minutes until I can listen to Malcolm's new songs.

When my shift finally ends at 1:00 a.m., I'm thankful my piece-of-crap car is old enough to have a CD player. I turn the key in the ignition and pop the disc in, smiling to myself as I roll down the windows and let Malcolm's voice and guitar spill out into the night. The first two songs are dark and confessional, and work well with just vocals and guitar. On the third track, I hear a drum and bass part in my head. This is a song in need of a band.

As I drive over the bridge that spans Barnegat Bay, the wind whips my hair and makes a loud *wah, wah, wah* in my ears. I turn up the music, breathe in the familiar mix of salt and fresh water, and take in the view. I love how the island looks from the bridge at night, a straight line of soft twinkling lights with one neon spike in the center, like a heartbeat on a monitor, marking the boardwalk and free fall tower.

I get through all five songs by the time I pull into my aunt's driveway of pebbles and crushed shells. When I walk in the door, my aunt's asleep on the couch with an unfinished glass of Pinot on the coffee table and CNN on the flat screen. She wakes up when I turn off the TV.

"Hey, Auntsie," I whisper. It's what I've always called her, a toddler's blend of *aunt* and *Annie*.

"How were the bands?" she mumbles.

"Good."

She always asks. Auntsie's a librarian, but she used to write music reviews for the local papers and even published her own zine. Her vinyl collection's as impressive as her personal library. There are floor-to-ceiling bookcases running the length of the bungalow's living room.

"You should come next Friday," I say.

She groans as she pushes herself up to a sitting position.

"Hear that? I'm making geriatric noises. I'm too old to rock."

Auntsie's forty-one, but like Caleb, and unlike Arnie, she can easily pass for much younger. Her round face is wrinkleless, and her arms and back are adorned with a good amount of ink.

Her long brown hair is currently in pigtails, making her look twelve, not middle-aged.

"You're not too old to rock. Caleb always asks for you." I give her a conspiratorial look.

She chuckles and shakes her head.

"Caleb. Nice guy. Too bad he's living in Neverland. We all can't survive on pixie dust."

Liam told me that before Caleb became a permanent fixture in the Jersey shore music scene, he toured with a band that opened for some big acts in the '90s. I know he and Auntsie have history, but she only ever talks about Caleb as a friend. I wave Malcolm's demo at her.

"Got some new tunes for you. I'll pass them along after I download them."

"Cool. I'm going to bed." She grabs her unfinished glass of wine then shuffles toward her bedroom in the back of the house. She stops short by the kitchen door and turns around.

"Remember, I have a summer reading thing all day at the library tomorrow and book club with the girls at night. You're on your own for dinner, unless you want to come along to book club."

"Nah, I'm good." I don't like to crash Auntsie's lifestyle any more than I already have. "I'll grab a slice on the boardwalk after work."

"Are you sure?"

I nod.

"Okay. Text me when you're in for the night, and don't forget we've got the shelter on Sunday."

"I won't." I tag along with Auntsie once a week to walk dogs at a no-kill shelter up the coast. She loves animals and I'm learning to.

Tomorrow I'm working the day shift at the Ben Franklin Five & Ten, a fixture in Lavallette for sixty-five years. With its red-and-white-striped awning, row of Adirondack chairs outside, and Yankee Candle smell inside, the store evokes happy memories of summers past and those yet to come.

The Ben Franklin is a sharp contrast to Keegan's, which smells like beer and decades-old cigarettes, but that's what I like about my jobs—the differences. The only complaint I have about my life at the shore, and it's more of a worry than complaint, is that the Ben Franklin is seasonal work. In the fall, if I can convince Auntsie and Mom to let me stay, I'll need to find another job to supplement my hours at Keegan's. That's in addition to coming up with the "solid life plan" Mom keeps going on about.

As opposed to an amorphous plan? I think to myself as I climb the narrow staircase to my second-floor bedroom. A solid life plan would be a lot easier if I had a solid life goal. I don't. I have no idea what I want. Never did. Even before losing Lynn, I was the kid who put her hand in the bag of Dum Dums lollipops and winged it. *You get what you get and you don't get upset.*

Of course, the exception may be this room. I wanted this room with its double bed, white eyelet curtains, and wicker furniture. It faces the water and smells like bay breeze, more so than the rest of the house. I've always loved it. But Mom took it whenever we visited, leaving Evie and I to share the room across the hall with bunk beds and a twin. I like that this room is mine now, even if it's only for a while.

I transfer Malcolm's demos to my laptop and phone. When I'm done, I change into the shorts I always sleep in and slip my bra out from under the tank top I was wearing under Auntsie's grunge shirt. I glance at my laptop and for, like, half a second, I consider taking one of those online career tests, but the thought sends me straight to bed. I slide between the cool sheets and lie there for a few seconds, listening to bay waves lap against the shore. Then I pop in my earbuds and listen to Malcolm's songs again.

When I get to the last track, the last song Malcolm played at Keegan's, I almost skip it, fearing it might trigger dreams of Lynn and the accident. But the safety of my bed and the lingering effects of the Xanax wrap me in the warm confidence and security I need to listen more closely. I imagine a keyboard and gospel choir backing Malcolm's raw vocals. I hear strings. A cello or maybe upright bass. I reach for the disc with his number. It's sitting on my nightstand.

Does he *really* want to know what I think?

I have more experience with tubas and trumpets than electric guitars. I tap Malcolm's number into my contacts, then allow my finger to hover over the message key, searching my mental catalog for musical lexicon that's hip and insightful. I pick honesty over pithy.

Love your songs

I hit send before considering whether or not this is a mistake. Seconds later I hear back.

Love? That's a strong word

They're strong songs

Hmm. I'd like to hear more. Meet at the beach tomorrow?

His question makes me sit up in bed.

Can't, gotta work

After?

Now I'm out of bed, pacing the hardwood floors. There's a thrumming inside my head jumbling my thoughts. What should I say? I guess I could say yes. He probably just wants to talk about his songs, no biggie. It's not me making something between us this time, right? He's the one who put himself out there. He gave me his songs. He asked me what *I* thought. And yeah, that part's a mystery because he probably knows a zillion musicians and who gives a monkey's ass what I think, but still. It would be rude to blow him off.

Six o'clock at the pizza place under the free fall tower?

Ack! What have I done? I flop back on my bed and wait

for his reply. Was I too specific? Does specific equal desperate? Should I have played it more like, "yeah, sure, whatev." I need to find girlfriends who can answer these types of questions for me. I wish I had Kiki's number. If she can handle Liam, she could handle this. But before I can have a mental breakdown over specificity vs. desperation, Malcolm texts back.

C u then

I turn my face into my pillow and smile, suddenly feeling too warm and wired to sleep. I pop back up and grab my laptop.

This is how it always begins with me, the weaver of fake, one-sided, obsessive relationships. I suffer heartbreak without ever actually having a boyfriend. And this time? This time I have too much damned material to work with. One internet search of Malcolm Trent and all the threads are there—the articles, the blog posts, the website, the music—enough to spin myself into a cocoon. If my sister were here, she'd organize an intervention. But she's not and I've got to stop. Or do I? He asked me to listen to his songs. He wants to meet me on the boardwalk tomorrow. Why would he go to all that trouble and then blow me off? I get up and turn on the window fan.

He wouldn't, I conclude.

I snap my laptop shut, lie back down, and let the fan's whirring lull me to sleep.

FIVE

I can't believe that motherfucker blew me off!

That's what's on replay in my head as I walk along the boardwalk the next evening with a giant pizza slice in one hand and an iced tea in the other.

Really? You can't believe some guy in a band blew you off?

The second voice clearly belongs to my sister.

She'd be right. I'm so stupid. I spent my entire eight-hour shift at the Ben Franklin allowing myself to believe something good was about to happen. I caught the anticipatory vibe that always emanates from the customers on the other side of the counter. They're all smiley and buoyant, stocking up on everything from beach umbrellas to those long kabob sticks for the grill. For them, the outside world with its long commutes and windowless cubicles fades away as soon as they drive over the bay bridge. By the time they hit the Ben Franklin, they're already wearing sunscreen, flip-flops, and happy faces.

For once, I wanted to feel that way too. I'm such a dumbass.

My eyes dart back and forth, searching for an empty bench where I can sit and watch the ocean and mentally beat myself up some more. That's when I see him. Malcolm.

He's shirtless and shoeless and staggering toward me. And yeah, I'm pissed and should be focused on ripping him a new one, but as we move toward each other, I find myself checking out his body. He's got a nice chest and broad shoulders. Strong arms too, and his thighs... What am I doing? This must be what it's like to have a penis.

He spots me and I freeze midstep. He draws closer still, squinting, until he's all up in my face, our noses practically touching. My cold drink sweats in my hand.

I take a step back. He smells like coconut suntan oil and rum.

"Sorry I'm late, Cat's Eye," he slurs.

"Quinn," I correct.

"Right." He takes a step back, puts his hands in his front pockets, and tries to steady himself. "I lost my friends."

Whoa. Is he talking about the accident, or...

"Do you mean, like, just now?"

He nods his head all innocent, and I glimpse that little boy again.

I give him an exaggerated once-over.

"Looks like you lost your clothes too."

"Ha. Ha." He nods his head toward the beach. "My stuff's on the blanket."

"Maybe your friends are there too. They probably went to the bathroom or to get some food or something."

"Mmm. Food sounds good. We've been drinking all day. That's why I'm so late."

"No?"

His eyes grow wide and he nods slowly.

"Yes." The alcohol has dulled his sarcasm detector.

Hands full, I motion toward an empty bench.

"Sit. I'll share my slice with you."

He puts one hand on his heart.

"You would do that?"

"Relax. It's pizza, not a kidney."

We sit down and I set the iced tea between us on the bench. With my plate on my lap, I try to rip the slice evenly without the cheese oozing off. I give him his half on the plate and keep mine on a napkin.

He folds his slice and takes a big bite. Two more like that and he'll be done.

"This is the best pizza ever," he says.

Ugh. This is not how I pictured tonight. I thought we'd walk around for a while, share funnel cake, talk about his songs.

Maybe ride the chairlift that takes you from the ride pier to the north end of the boardwalk. But clearly, I'm not meant to act like a tourist today. He's stupid drunk and I'm suddenly worried.

"How'd you get here?"

"Drove," he says through a big mouthful.

"Your own car?"

"Whose car would I take?"

"No, I meant—" I hand him my uneaten pizza. "Take this. You need to put something else in your stomach."

He shakes his head, but I insist.

"Take it. I'll get myself another slice. Be right back."

I leave him on the bench and weave through the crowd, an odd mixture of families and freaks. I'm not much of a swimmer or sun worshipper, but I've always loved the boardwalk with its neon glow and carnival vibe. If heaven exists, I'm certain it smells like cotton candy and fried dough.

I return with a slice for me and water for Malcolm, expecting to find him where I left him, but only an oil-stained paper plate remains. He's gone. And he took my iced tea with him. Bastard.

I slump down on the bench, take a bite of my slice, and wonder what I'm going to do with the rest of my night. Like Malcolm, I'm short on friends. I love living with my aunt—and my life here in general—but I don't have anyone to spend time with, besides Auntsie, that is. Kiki keeps saying I should hang out with her and Lucy, but I dunno.

At home I've got my sister and her friends, and Marissa and Priya, who took me on as their third wheel after Lynn died. But Marissa, Priya, and I have never been all that close and come next month, they'll both be leaving for college anyway. Marissa to Syracuse, and Priya to Delaware. And me? I'll be walking shelter dogs and waiting on the Spoon Man and Arnie. But I'm okay with that because Lynn should have been on her way to Princeton or Harvard, or some other fancy school. She was the super smart one and I was the one with dumb and dangerous ideas. I twist my cuff bracelet and stare at the ocean.

"Is anybody sitting here?" a mom with two ice-cream-cone-toting kids asks.

I shake my head. "Nobody's sitting there."

The kids plop down and the mom stays standing. I scooch closer to the end to give them more room, then root through my bag for my quilted froggy-face change purse filled with quarters. Might as well play Skee-ball. Where the heck is it? I peer inside. Why don't purses come with refrigerator-like lights that flick on as soon as they're open? Panic rises. I don't care about the quarters, but the purse belonged to Lynn.

After she died, her mom asked me to come over and look through her things. She wanted me to take some of her clothes and anything else I wanted, which I found weird and sad and confusing but I knew from the look on Lynn's mother's face that I had to take something. In the end, I chose the change purse, because it had cute googly eyes and I knew Lynn loved it. Even though it was kiddish, she brought it to school every day filled with change for the vending machine.

I rummage more frantically until finally, my hand finds it and I exhale.

"I'm back."

I look up to find Malcolm standing in front of me. Drinking my iced tea.

"Bet you thought you lost me too," he says.

I tighten my grip on Froggy and ignore the prickly sensation moving down my spine.

"I didn't think I lost you."

He's wearing a hoodie and Vans, and has a large beach towel slung over one shoulder. He plops down next to me, squeezing himself between me and the kids. We're so close our shoulders touch. Malcolm yawns. It's loud and embarrassing and I sense the mom's disapproval as keenly as if she were my own mother.

"I'm soooo tired. I could sleep right here," he says.

"Let me drive you home."

He shakes his head.

"I don't want to leave my car."

He slumps sideways, his body getting heavier on mine until one of my butt cheeks slips off the bench. Next thing I know, he rests his cheek against the top of my head. Whoa, space invader!

That's enough. I shift out from under him and stand up. He almost falls over and the mom shoots him a look.

"How 'bout you come hang at my aunt's house for a while? It's not far. I'll drive you back to your car later."

"You sure?" he asks.

I nod, offer my hand, and pull him off the bench. He steadies himself, then puts his arm around my shoulder. His sweatshirt smells like the ocean. I wrap my arm around his waist to counterbalance his drunken heft, and we walk along like that until we reach the metered lot at the boardwalk's end where I parked. I have to pry his arm off me to make him let go. Another unromantic evening, like the one with my emotionally stunted student teacher who used me as a coda to his band geek youth.

"What am I doing?" I whisper to myself. *Malcolm's not another nobody. He needs help*, I think. I'll sober him up, tell him what I thought of his songs, and send him on his way.

"Buckle up," I say out loud, more to myself than to Malcolm, before I put the car in reverse and pull out of my spot. This could be an interesting ride.

SIX

Back at Auntsie's, Malcolm sobers up quick when he lays eyes on her turntable and vinyl collection.

"Are these yours?"

He's so impressed I almost lie.

"My aunt's."

"I worked in a record store in high school. I have a decent vinyl collection myself."

What does he do now? I wonder.

He brushes his fingertips down the album spines, arranged alphabetically by genre, and stops when he gets to the Ramones. With bloodshot eyes, he asks, "Can I?"

"As long as you don't take the record out of the sleeve and you put it back exactly where you found it. Auntsie's very particular."

He nods, slides out *Road to Ruin*, and holds it like a thin sheet of glass. Auntsie would be proud. He studies the cartoon drawing on the front, then flips the album over and squints as he reads. The sun is setting, and we're both wrapped in shadows. I flick on the table lamp and he looks up at me.

"Do you think she'll play it for me sometime?"

I'm struck by his assumption that he'll be back. That after the alcohol evaporates from his pores and I drop him at his car, he won't drive away and never want to see me again.

"I'm sure she will. As long as you don't mind hearing about how she scored an interview with Joey Ramone for her zine."

"You know that's cool, right?"

"Oh, I know it's cool. She reminds me every time she tells the story. That and the one about how she interviewed Moe Tucker from the Velvet Underground."

"Have you always lived with your aunt?"

I shake my head.

"Just since June. I live with my mom and sister in North Jersey."

"Your dad?"

I point to my one blue eye.

"DNA suggests I have one, but I don't remember him. He left when I was two and my sister was a newborn."

"There are worse things. My parents live to make each other miserable. If they weren't in business together, I have a feeling they both would have walked away a long time ago. Some people are only meant to be together for a short time and a specific purpose."

"Agreed. I've got no complaints. You can't miss something you've never had, and my mom's amazing. I'm the one who's impossible to live with."

"That why you're here?"

I nod.

"We haven't talked since Fourth of July weekend. We text. We don't talk. It's my fault though. I screwed up."

He tilts his head. "Is this about your best friend?"

Why did I ever tell him that? Why do I tell him anything? I barely know this guy.

I step toward him, take the album from his hand, and slide it onto the shelf where it belongs. I pretend to straighten the stack so I don't have to see his face. I sense his eyes on me though.

"That was the screwup that started it all. This latest was in June and it wasn't that bad."

His hand touches my back, between my shoulder blades, and I flinch.

"Wanna talk about it?"

I glance at him over my shoulder. "Which one?"

"Either? Group therapy made me a good listener." He laughs, but there's a heaviness to it.

I turn and face him.

"Did it also make you a good sharer?"

"Not so much. I'd rather stick pins in my eyes or take a cold shower."

"We're all out of pins, but you can take a cold shower if you want. Or lukewarm, whatever. You know, so you don't smell like a Piña Colada if a cop stops you."

He grins. "I smell like a Piña Colada?"

"There are worse things."

I take him upstairs, hand him two towels for extra coverage, and point him toward the bathroom.

I wait until I hear water running, then step into my room and pick up my drumsticks. I don't have real drums here, only an electronic tabletop set that I'm using to teach myself to play a kit. Clarinet was my first instrument in fifth grade band, but I played it like a honking goose and switched to drums in sixth grade. Three years later, after Lynn died, I was thankful I'd opted for the snare drum. I wanted to smash things all the time. Her death changed the way I played. Drums calmed my brain and became a conduit for my rage.

I sit down at my desk, pick up my sticks, and start with some practice exercises. Rudiments. I play singles, move to doubles, then switch to paradiddles, which are a combination of both. My muscle memory takes over and my hands move faster and faster. *Right, left, right, right. Left, right, left, left.* After a warm-up, I put on my headphones and cue up Malcolm's songs. A drum part for the third track came to me, and I want to try to work it out. After a while, I lose myself to the rhythm, forgetting where I am and that Malcolm Trent is in my shower until he's standing in front of me in a towel. I jump.

"How long have you been there?"

"Sorry. When I got out of the shower, the bathroom was steamy. I opened the door for some air and I heard... You play drums?" he asks.

"Snare. In the marching band. Not very rock and roll."

"A girl that plays drums? That's the definition of rock and roll. What were you listening to?"

"Uh. Your songs? I had an idea for that third track..."

I'm trying to keep my eyes on his face, but his chest is in my line of sight and there are these tiny rivulets of water gliding along his skin... I drop my sticks and stand.

"Why don't you change in here? There's no ventilation in that bathroom. I'll wait downstairs."

"Sure?"

"Yeah, yeah of course. I should have offered before."

"I won't be long."

"Take your time."

Downstairs, I remember to text my aunt to let her know I'm home, omitting the part about not being alone. As soon as Malcolm's dressed, I'll take him back to his car and then I really will be alone.

I plop down on the overstuffed couch, flip through channels, and try not to think about Malcolm Trent, naked in my room. I told him to take his time, but he's been up there for freaking ever. What's he doing? He wouldn't go through my stuff, would he? Not that there's much to see aside from the books, drums, and bed.

I move to the bottom of the steps and listen for a door opening, padding feet. I hear nothing. When I can't take it anymore, I creep upstairs and rap on my closed door.

"Malcolm?"

I wait a few seconds and when I get no answer, I open the door a crack and look in.

Malcolm Trent, still wearing only a towel, is asleep on my bed.

SEVEN

I shut the door. This is a new one, even for me.
Irrespective of what half my town thought of me after the band
teacher/Jaws of Life debacle, I've never had a boy in my bedroom
or been alone with a boy in his. I grab a quilt from the bedroom
across the hall, then quietly open the door to my room again.
Malcolm's back is to me, and I'm hoping to God that towel is
closed as I tiptoe around the double bed. Through squinty eyes, I
drape the quilt over him.

What should I do now? I watch Malcolm for a few seconds,
not creepy-long but maybe longer than I should, and think about
his songs. The hurt inside him seems to understand the hurt
inside me. I'm about to leave when his hand reaches out and
brushes my fingertips. I freeze.

"Stay," he says.

Then, without opening his eyes, he lifts the covers and makes room beside him.

All the reasons I shouldn't climb in next to him loop in my brain. He's drunk, I'm vulnerable. He's a loincloth away from full-frontal nudity. My aunt will kill me. I hardly know him. I'll get hurt. He's drunk. Oh yeah, I said that. I don't know if it's my heart or body guiding me, but it doesn't matter because neither listens to my head as I step out of my flip-flops, ease myself onto the bed, and lay down beside him spoon-style. Malcolm wraps the quilt and his arm around me in one motion. My body tenses and he responds by pressing his lips to the back of my head and whispering into my hair.

"We'll just sleep. I promise. Just sleep." His beard brushes my cheek as he leans up to kiss my temple. "Okay?"

I give a slight nod and ease my body against his. His hand travels down my arm, until his fingertips rest in my palm. With his thumb, he traces the edge of my bracelet.

"Souvenir," I say. I'm not sure if he hears.

"Of?"

"A terrible year."

He gives a sleepy laugh. "The Sundays."

He knows his '90s alt rock. I'm about to say so, but his deep, even breaths tell me he's already fallen back to sleep. I lie there for a few minutes as my angels and demons duke it out. The press of his body against me, the rhythm of his rising and falling chest, lull me into a false sense of security. I like this unfamiliar feeling of someone holding on to me. *This isn't real. He isn't mine*, I tell myself as I stare out the open window at the moon. And yet, I can't pry myself away. Whatever this is right now, this minute, I want it. A warmth is seeping into the cold hollow inside me and I don't want it to end.

I awake to a yellow glow in my window and a seagull laughing. *Rooster of the sea*, I think and smile before I'm hit with the smell of coffee and a scary realization. I fell asleep! Malcolm's hand is on my hip, his legs are tangled up with mine, and his towel has slipped off. *Shit! Do I hear footsteps?* I untie myself from Malcolm, and slink out of bed without waking him. Auntsie's putting a foot on the bottom step when I walk into the hallway and close the door behind me.

"Quinn, baby! Good, you're already dressed. I was coming up to get you." Her voice booms. *Oh geez.* "Ready to do God's work?"

She means it ironically. A lapsed Catholic, Auntsie likes to call our Sundays at the shelter "church."

I scoot down the steps to meet her, and pray Malcolm's still sleeping. She keeps talking. "I fixed your coffee the way you like it. We have time for a quick cup before we go. We'll get breakfast after. How about Denny's? I could go for Moons Over My Hammy."

She loves to use the actual menu names when she orders.

"Whataya think? We haven't been there yet."

Has she always been this loud? I link arms with her and usher her toward the kitchen, but she breaks away from me and moves toward the steps.

"Just a second. I want to pull the sheets off the bed in the guest room. Your sister and her friend are coming next weekend and—"

I jump in front of her. "I can do that. Go have your coffee." I walk backward up the steps, my hands clutching the railings on either side of me, so she can't get by. "It's no trouble. I-I got this," I stammer.

She tries to duck under my arm, so I sit on the steps and full-on body block her.

She narrows her eyes and puts her hands on her hips.

"Why are you sweating?"

"It's hot?" It is. But it's no use. She knows me too well. My shoulders slump in resignation. "There's a naked boy in my bed and before you say anything, I did not have sex with him."

I hope she finds my bluntness funny, but I can see she's not amused.

"Kitchen. Now."

Crap. Here we go again.

EIGHT

Auntsie sets her coffee down and crosses her arms over her chest. Her expression says, *This ought to be good.*

"It's not what you think."

"Oh good, because I was thinking there's a naked boy in your bed."

"Okay, yeah. There's that. But it sounds worse than it is. I met him on the boardwalk and he was drunk, and I didn't want him to drive home."

"Oh, okay. My bad. You're right. Picking up drunken strangers on the boardwalk isn't so bad. I think they give Girl Scouts badges for that."

My heart races. I'm saying this all wrong.

"He wasn't a stranger! I met him for the first time at Keegan's. Malcolm Trent. I told you about his songs, remember? I brought him back here to sober up. After he showered, he fell asleep in my bed. I'm sorry. I should have told you he was here. I wanted to. But then I fell asleep too."

Auntsie sucks in her breath. "Quinn. You're going to get us both in trouble. Your mother trusted me. *Me*. The immature aunt who can't even keep a cactus alive."

Mom always says her sister doesn't "do" adult.

"I'm not in trouble. You're not in trouble. There is no trouble." I can't stand the thought of my aunt looking at me the way Mom did after the incident with my student teacher made the local news. "It's not like that. Nothing happened. I swear."

Auntsie raises a dubious eyebrow.

"Okay, I shouldn't have let him crash here. I realize that now. It's not going to happen again."

"You got that right. It can never happen again. Not in this house. Not on my watch. Not if you want to keep living here. You're here because your heart needs fixing. The last thing you need is some washed-up rocker messing with your head."

Her cheeks flush and her voice approaches a yell. She never yells.

"He's not washed up or messing with my head. And Mr. G did not break my heart."

Auntsie gives me a pointed stare. "I never said he was the one who did."

She sighs. "Aww, Quinn baby, for the record, there's nothing wrong with having sex with the right guy. But you have a knack for picking losers. You deserve better. You deserve someone who will love you all the way."

"Are you quoting Barry Manilow? Because you sound like Barry Manilow. Or worse, Evie and Mom."

Her face softens.

"Funny, everyone always says I sound like you."

It's true. People compare us all the time. Tell us we look alike and how I could have been Auntsie's daughter. I don't mind the comparison, but at times it makes both Mom and Auntsie feel bad, for different reasons.

"I'm sorry," I say.

"Yeah, I'm sorry too."

What does she mean by that? Is she sorry she let me live here? Sorry she believed in me? I thought she and I were moving past this awful moment, that she'd come back to my side, but I thought wrong. She takes her keys off the hook and grabs her handbag in a huff.

"I'm going to the shelter. I want that boy gone by the time I get back."

Mom was wrong. She does do adult.

"I'll wake him right now. I'll go with you like we planned."

She puts a hand on my shoulder. "I think we both need some time to ourselves."

She says it softly, nicely, but it still stings like a slap. First Mom, now my aunt.

"Oh, okay, well…give Reggie an extra treat from me."

Reggie is this Chihuahua-Papillon mix. He's blind in one eye and missing a bunch of teeth, so his tongue perpetually hangs out one side of his mouth. I brush him every week and keep hoping someone will appreciate his awesome ugliness.

"I will," Auntsie says.

I watch Auntsie leave through the back door then turn toward the living room. When I round the corner, Malcolm is sitting on the bottom step.

"Hey. So I'm gonna head out now."

I panic. "You heard?"

He nods. "Thanks for having my back, by the way."

My mind does a rapid rewind. I try to piece together what was said.

"Who's Mr. G?" Malcolm asks.

"Nobody."

"Sounds more like a weatherman than a nobody."

Malcolm slaps his knees and stands. "Look, about yesterday. I'm sorry if I… I don't usually drink like that. Your aunt's right about me. I shouldn't have—"

He closes his eyes and exhales, like he's pained by what he's about to say. I know this moment. I *live* in this moment. Most recently with Mr. G after we were rescued from our date by the fire department. *I have to think about my career, my reputation. Blah. Blah.* He should have thought of that before he handed a Blue Moon to an underage drinker. Whatever. I know when I'm about to hear that spending time with me was a mistake, so I don't give Malcolm a chance. I don't know if we'll ever be more, or even friends, but right now, I can't be his mistake.

"Look, don't worry about my aunt. She doesn't know you. She was angry with me. You hungry? I'm hungry. There's a bagel place around the corner. You've gotta eat, right? I'll drive you back to your car afterward. Promise. I'll tell you all about Mr. G. and we can talk about your songs. We never got the chance to talk about them. I have all these ideas, especially for the one you played at Keegan's. I'm totally hearing keys and gospel backing vocals on that one. After that, you can leave and we'll pretend last night never happened…"

I take a deep breath, prepared to go on sounding desperate and stupid and hating myself for trying to claw my way from awkward to normal, but then Malcolm takes my face in his hands and kisses me on the lips. Softly, gently.

"Thank you," he says.

I manage to regain enough breath to ask, "For kissing you?"

"For saving me. Last night. From myself."

I wave my hand. "It was nothing."

"It wasn't nothing. Seriously, I owe you."

"Buy me a bagel and we'll call it even."

He motions toward the door. "Lead the way."

NINE

We sit under the gazebo by the bay, eating
everything bagels with extra veggie cream cheese and drinking
coffee. I tell him about the crush that nearly killed me. How
my student teacher wooed me with his cheesy note and how
our one and only date consisted of Blue Moons in his car in
the park.

"I don't even like beer."

"At least it wasn't piss water," Malcolm offers.

"Yeah, well, too bad for me we parked under a giant oak.
Out of nowhere there was this crazy thunderstorm with wind and
hail. A huge branch broke off and crashed onto his car's roof.
Glass shattered. Rainwater seeped in. Good thing we were in the
back seat and he was trying to convince me to have sex with him

at the time. If not, we would have been crushed to death." I raise my arms half-heartedly and do a mock jeer. "Silver lining, yay! We even made News 12. Guess I wasted my fifteen minutes of fame on Mr. G."

I tear off a piece of bagel and pop it into my mouth, chewing slowly as I stare off into the distance at two WaveRunners speeding by. The sad part is I thought I saw a kindred spirit in Mr. G—a socially awkward band geek who felt music as deeply as I did.

"You know that guy was an asshole, right? What kind of prick tries to date a student?" Malcolm's anger surprises me. "He was a teacher. And you're a minor."

I take a slow sip of my caramel latte, thankful the transition lenses in my awesomely ugly glasses are hiding my eyes.

"He was a *student* teacher and I'm eighteen. Closer to nineteen."

"Yeah, but still. A guy like that. He shouldn't be allowed around kids. I'm twenty and consider any girl in high school completely off-limits."

"I could have kept my clothes on. Maybe then he would have called afterward."

Malcolm touches my chin. At first I think he's wiping off some stray cream cheese, but then I realize he's being nice.

"Quinn, look at me. You have nothing to be ashamed of, and anyone who has anything to say about that can fuck off."

He's right, isn't he? For the first time since the whole shitty incident, someone sees that a shitty thing happened *to* me, not *because of* me.

"Thank you."

He sips his black coffee. "For what?"

"Being on my side."

"There's no other side to be on here. You did nothing wrong."

I shrug. "Easy for you to say. You should have seen the look on my mother's face." I shake my head. "Let's not talk about me anymore. Let's talk about your songs."

He smiles. "You said you loooved them."

I nudge his arm. "Don't mock me."

"They're the first songs I've written in two years. Rehab can be a real time suck."

He throws the information out there casually, and I try not to overreact.

"You mentioned group therapy last night."

He waves one hand at me.

"Got addicted to prescription painkillers after I broke my hand. From there I tried heroin. Snorted it. No needles. I never thought—"

A Nerf football rolls into the gazebo and hits Malcolm in the foot. I'm thankful for the interruption because I don't know how to respond when someone reveals something this mind-blowingly huge.

Malcolm picks up the ball and tosses it back to the kids

playing catch on the bay beach. Families with young children are setting up for the day; every swing is filled.

"Yesterday, you were drinking. Is that—"

He shakes his head. "I shouldn't have done that. I'm only sixth months clean. But I was hanging with some old high school friends, guys I was friends with before…everything. They snuck a huge thermos of rum and Coke onto the beach. I didn't want to be a guy with dead friends and a failed music career."

Is he *still* six months clean? How does alcohol affect his pill addiction and sobriety? It's almost like he sees the questions in my eyes and doesn't want to answer. Without looking at me, he crumples his paper bag and bagel wrapper and gets up to throw them out with his empty cup.

"You didn't fail. Something terrible happened to you," I say when he sits down beside me again, hunched over with his elbows on his knees.

"Something terrible happened to my friends. Me? I'm twenty years old working part-time at a gas station when I'm not making coffee at NA meetings, sponging off my parents, and basically blowing my second chance."

"You're not blowing anything. You've got five incredible songs that you need to do something with."

He looks at me and smiles. "Like hire a gospel choir and pianist?"

I blush. "That was stupid. I shouldn't have said that. There are people out there who can give you a better opinion. I just know I love your songs."

"The gospel choir isn't a terrible idea."

"You're just saying that."

"Maybe."

He gives me a side squeeze, then lets his arm drop and stands up.

"Time to go?" I ask.

"Got to call my sponsor. Plus, your aunt was crystal clear about wanting me gone. If she hates me, she'll never let you be part of my plan."

"What plan?"

He raises a finger to his lips. "Shh. It's got to stay a secret."

"For how long?"

"Until I work out the details. Don't worry. When I do, you'll be one of the first to know."

We walk back to my aunt's to get my car, and from there I drive him to his. A black pickup. It looks new.

"Nice ride," I say when I pull up alongside it.

"Insurance money." He imitates my earlier mock cheer. "Silver lining, yay."

I give him a half grin, unsure what to say as the silence lasts a beat too long. Then Malcolm rests one hand on my shoulder, gives it a nearly imperceptible squeeze, and opens the car door.

"Later, Cat's Eye. I'll be in touch."

TEN

"Q!"

When I walk into Keegan's almost a week later, Liam rushes toward me with a deranged smile on his face. To be fair, it probably only seems deranged because Liam never smiles. He's a smirker and not prone to outward displays of emotion. That's why it's even more shocking when he scoops me into a gravity-defying hug and spins me around. He's stronger than he looks for a short-ish guy.

"What the hell, Liam? Did you have dental work done this morning?" Nitrous oxide is the only explanation for why he's laughing like a fool. I slap his back. "Put me down!"

Liam stops short and releases me with a thunk. "If I was sure Kiki wouldn't kill me, I'd kiss you."

I take two steps back. "Don't worry about Kiki, worry about me. I don't want your lips anywhere near me."

Liam laughs again, and I'm beginning to wonder if he needs medical attention. He puts me in a friendly headlock, if there is such a thing, and plants a kiss on top of my head with a "mwah" sound.

I push him away. "Enough! You. Are. Freaking. Me. Out. What's going on?"

"I don't know what you said to Malcolm, but thank you!"

"For what?"

"He called and asked if I wanted to try out for his band. I met him at a rehearsal studio earlier today to jam."

Ahh. That explains it. After not hearing from Malcolm since Sunday, he texted me yesterday asking if I knew anyone who played guitar.

"I just mentioned your name and gave him your number," I say.

"Well, I'm in! He wants me to record his new songs with him at this totally pro studio. I have to learn all the guitar parts for the originals plus two covers, 'Sunday Bloody Sunday' and 'Seven Nation Army.' Both are pretty basic."

I slouch against the bar. Is this Malcolm's secret plan? What happened to me being one of the first to know? I guess technically I am "one of" the first to know, but I'm disappointed because I thought I ranked ahead of Liam. More importantly, I assumed I was somehow involved.

"Rehearsals start next week. He booked studio time in late August," Liam continues. It's the happiest I've ever seen him. I guess that's what happens when you have something to look forward to.

"August, huh? That's great."

Is it great? What's so great about Malcolm's secret plan to record his songs with a random guitarist I recommended?

"You've got to learn the drum parts for those songs too," Liam says.

Wait. What?

"What are you talking about?"

"Sorry, I figured you knew. Malcolm said you already tried out."

"I'm in his band?"

"Looks like it. He mentioned he wants you to learn the drum parts for the U2 and White Stripes songs too."

Hmph. Would have been nice to be asked.

"I can't be in his band." I reach for the bulk-sized box of trail mix and start filling bowls. "Even if I could learn all those drum parts, I won't be good anytime soon. I can't do it."

Liam walks away from me and ducks behind the bar. "You can and you will. That's what YouTube is for," he calls out while bending down to retrieve something. When he pops back up he hands me a large manila envelope. "Malcolm gave me this to give to you."

"What is it?"

"Not sure. My X-ray vision's a bit wonky lately, but if I had to guess, it feels like a book."

I resist the urge to remind Liam he's a dick and open the package in front of him.

"Superman's got nothing on you," I say when I spill the contents.

Inside the envelope is a copy of Patti Smith's memoir *Just Kids* and a note that begins: *Something artsier for your feminist collection.* The note also says he's scheduled a rehearsal studio for next week, Thursday night, and concludes with, *Want to be in my band?*

Guess he did ask. I text him immediately.

It can't work.

Y?

My aunt.

I'll talk to her.

Drums?

Got 'em.

I've never played a real kit

You'll learn. I'll teach you.

Record the drum parts yourself then

Don't want to. And I can't play both drums and bass live.

Live?

I'll explain when I see you.

I turn to Liam. "What did Malcolm say about playing live?"

"That's the best part! He wants us to do a gig here on Labor Day. He's talking to Caleb about it. Andrew should be back from camp by then. I gotta text him. You'll finally get to meet him!"

After Liam mentions the gig, all I hear is *Andrew, blah, blah, blah*. Because, I have to play live?! I guess technically I've done that lots of times. But I was unrecognizable in my huge plumed hat amid 150 marching band members. I have to admit though—having an audience for my occasional drum solo did give me a rush. And mastering a full kit could be fun. It's what I wanted before I even met Malcolm. This will give me a reason to do it. Maybe I can even save up to buy my own. I would love the green sparkle kind. I bite my lower lip and picture it. The drums. A band. All of it. But if I'm going to get my aunt and mom on board, there will have to be parameters. I want Malcolm and Liam to take me seriously.

It's taking me too long to respond, apparently. Malcolm texts a row of question marks. I reply.

If I do this, you have to promise to keep your drunken ass out of my bed

What if I'm sober???

Malcolm!

Promise

And you can't try to kiss me

Then don't try to save me

I'll have my lawyer draw up the papers

You have a lawyer?

I don't even have real drums

So you're in?

I'm in

And just like that, me, the drumless drummer, agrees to join Malcolm Trent's band. Now to figure out how I'm going to explain it to Auntsie.

ELEVEN

"**Absolutely not.**"

That's what Auntsie says when I rouse her from her usual spot on the couch and tell her about Malcolm's plan.

It was reassuring to see her there when I walked in. We haven't seen too much of each other since Sunday, and I was beginning to think *I* was the reason she'd been leaving the house early and coming home late every night this week.

"He wants to talk to you about it," I say.

"When?"

"Our first practice is supposed to be Thursday night. Before then I guess?"

"Tell him to come to dinner on Sunday. I'll make linguine and clam sauce."

Somehow I envisioned this talk sans pasta. But I get it. Her house, her rules.

"Okay." I hold up the book Malcolm gave me in an attempt to win him more points. "Look, he left this at Keegan's for me."

Auntsie swings her legs off the couch and sits up. "Patti Smith, huh? I love that book."

I smile inside and stop twisting my bracelet. "You'll like him. I know you will."

"Your sister can help me render my verdict on Sunday."

My sister?

"You're inviting Evie to dinner?"

"She'll already be here. Remember? She's coming tomorrow morning with her friend Kate."

That's right. I totally forgot. "How're they getting here?" Translation: *Is Mom coming?*

"Kate's sister Ashley is dropping them off. Your mom's picking them up Wednesday."

Mom's a paralegal for a law firm. She works a gazillion hours when one of her attorneys is on trial, but her bosses are also very generous with the comp time. Especially in the summer, which is good for my sister. Evie will be a junior in the fall, but kids in New Jersey can't drive without a parent until they're seventeen.

Maybe I can work a double shift at the Ben Franklin on Wednesday.

Auntsie reads my mind. "You and your mother are going to have to talk sooner or later."

"Why? Her icy tone and my sarcasm translate fine via text."

Auntsie sighs. "What about Malcolm? She needs to know."

I panic. "About the bed thing?"

"God no! Let's leave that out. About joining his band."

Phew. "So you're okay with it?"

"We'll find out Sunday, won't we?"

I guess we will.

Upstairs I flip through the book Malcolm gave me. I can tell by the cracked spine and handwritten notes in the margins that it's been read carefully. I normally don't approve of defacing books, but in this case, I can't resist following Malcolm's breadcrumbs. Like listening to his music, it's another chance to poke around in his mind. So I start reading.

It begins with a death. Three pages in, Malcolm has made a thin black line under the words *providence determined how I would say goodbye.* I keep reading, as much to see what happens as how Malcolm reacted to it. I make it to page twenty-five before I get tired and start to read with one eye, resting my brown eye first before switching to the blue. But I fight exhaustion and keep reading because I'm afraid that when I fall asleep, I'll dream about Lynn.

Sometimes I dream about the accident, the parts I remember anyway. The soul-piercing squeal of brakes, the thud of metal hitting metal. Other times, I dream Lynn is alive. I run into her unexpectedly in some everyday mundane location: the band room at school, our kitchen, the mall. The places change, but one piece remains constant. I'm always carrying something heavy; a bass drum, a case of water, bulky packages. She always smiles, holds out her arms, and says the same thing: "Here, let me help you with that."

TWELVE

Evie arrives in dramatic style the next morning, pouncing on my bed like Tigger in a bounce house. I panic for a moment, not knowing where I am. But then my heart slows when I realize I'm at Auntsie's and I didn't dream at all last night.

"You're missing a perfect beach day!"

I cover my head with a pillow. She's the one who's all about the sun and the sand. Not me. I'm about places I can wear my Doc Martens and cutoff overalls in the summer. I reach for my phone and drag it under the pillow with me.

"Evie, it's not even seven! The sun is barely awake."

"Kate's sister wanted to get an early start. It's her only day off this week, so our plan is to stay on the beach until dark. Are you coming with us?"

I toss my pillow aside and sit up. "Can't. I'm working at the Ben Franklin today."

Her lower lip curls. "Bummer. Boardwalk tonight? I want to ride the new free fall tower. Have you done it yet?"

I shake my head. "Not yet. It's not as tall as the old one."

The free fall tower, Jet Star roller coaster, and the old Ferris wheel were all victims of Superstorm Sandy. It's the second summer since the storm, and although some things on the shore are getting better, they'll never be the same.

Evie jumps off the bed. "We stopped at McDonald's. I got you hotcakes and hash browns."

Ever since we were little kids, Evie's been dreaming up ways to lure me out of bed at the crack of dawn on weekends. She was always like: *I heard a noise in the kitchen. I need help with the toaster oven. That band you like is on the morning show.*

But she's finally learning. I'll always get up for hotcakes and hash browns.

"What the hell are you wearing?" Evie screams when I enter the kitchen.

I look down at my cotton shorts and tee.

"Pajamas?"

"I meant on your face," Evie says.

I adjust my frames. I forgot. Evie hasn't seen me in my new glasses.

"They were Grammy's," I say.

Evie huffs. "I can tell. Even she wears contacts now, you know."

I move to the counter and pour myself a cup of coffee. "I know." Grammy said the contacts improved her golf game. She and Pop play all the time now that they live in Florida. Even before the contacts, she always wore snazzy frames. Auntsie said the ones I'm wearing were Grammy's in high school.

"Honestly, Quinn. It's like you go out of your way to make yourself unapproachable."

Ashley and Kate offer me sympathetic looks.

"Hey," I say and smile to both of them. They give me a "hey" back.

If I'd known my hotcakes came with psychoanalysis instead of syrup, I would have stayed in bed. Wasn't she the one who thought I needed protection from The Nobodies?

"I'm wearing glasses, not barbed wire," I snap back.

"And what about this boy?"

"What boy?"

"Auntsie says there's a boy coming to dinner tomorrow."

Oh lord. Sometimes I forget that inside Evie's petite sixteen-year-old body is a forty-something PTA mom dying to bust out.

I shoot Auntsie a look.

"What? All I said was you're having a friend over."

"Did you tell her why?" I ask.

"Nope. Figured I'd leave that to you, Taylor Hawkins."

I look at my aunt smiling smugly in her Foo Fighters T-shirt, and wonder if she's ever going to join this millennium. I should point out that her Foo Fighters drummer reference is lost on everyone but me, but why bother.

"I'll never be as good as Taylor," I mumble instead. I launch into my explanation of Malcolm's plan for me to record some songs with him. I include his backstory, the tragic accident, and hopes for a comeback. For obvious reasons, I leave out his stint in rehab and the bit about my bed. Kate and Ashley are sorry for his loss—who isn't?—and curious about his music. But Evie looks worried.

"You didn't kiss him, did you?"

"*Pfff*. No!"

"Quinnnn?" She drags out my name like I'm a puppy caught chewing the rug.

I bite my lower lip. "Okay, so what if I did? It doesn't matter anyway because we agreed it can never happen again. Not if we're going to be working together."

"Wish I could spend my summer in a rock band," Kate says through a mouthful of Egg McMuffin.

"Mmm hmm," Ashley agrees.

Evie's "nobody" detector must sound like an air-raid siren in her head.

"I'm pretty sure this is not what Mom had in mind when she said you needed a solid life plan by the end of the summer."

It probably isn't. But short of becoming Evie, I'm not sure what Mom wants from me. I don't say that though. It wouldn't be fair. Evie's not a good girl because she's trying to make me look bad. I recognize playing music with Malcolm and Liam isn't exactly going to make me look *good*, but the idea stirs an unfamiliar excitement that I'm unwilling to let go of. I can't remember the last time I looked forward to anything.

I grab my hash browns and stand to go.

"I've got to shower before work. Have fun at the beach today." Then I retreat to the safety of my room, undeterred by Evie's lack of support. Tomorrow's dinner with Malcolm should be interesting.

THIRTEEN

Malcolm arrives on Sunday afternoon bearing vinyl for my aunt and drums for me.

"Figured I'd bring the hi-hat in now. The rest is in my truck."

I take the hi-hat, which looks like two cymbals facing each other on a stick, and set them down by the door.

"Come in," I say without making eye contact. My mouth's been stricken with a sudden dryness that's making my lips stick to my teeth. Why am I so nervous? It's like he's meeting my father for the first time, even though Auntsie's a woman, and I've never even met my father, not really. I'm glad Evie and Kate ditched an early Sunday dinner in favor of more beach time.

"You look nice," Malcolm says as he leans in to hug me. He *smells* nice, like soap and cologne instead of a cocktail or tobacco.

"You too," I say as I smooth my navy blue cotton sundress. I'm wearing it with combat boots, to make sure it doesn't look like I'm trying too hard, which, I am. I even scrubbed twice with shower gel so I'd smell like "Honolulu Sunshine" not wet shelter dog. Auntsie and I worked a double shift this morning walking, feeding, and beautifying two pit bull mixes, a beagle, and my Reggie.

But if I'm trying hard, so is he.

He's wearing a cool vintage bowling shirt with the name "Hank" stitched over the left breast pocket, and just-right fitting jeans with a tear over one knee. His beard looks more coiffed than usual, and his still-wet hair has been swept away from his face.

"This is for you," Malcolm says to Auntsie as he hands her an album.

Auntsie holds it up. "*Revolver?* Thank you."

"I tried to find something alt-rock, but then I figured, you could never go wrong with the Beatles, right? I really like the cover art."

Auntsie studies the album. The jacket has a cool pencil drawing of Paul, John, George, and Ringo and that whole '60s psychedelic vibe going on. She smiles, but in a way that makes me think she's saying "suck-up" to herself.

"Very cool, thank you. You guys mind if I play it?" She's being nice, but not her usual warm self.

"Promise to play the Ramones next?" Malcolm asks.

"You got it." He's speaking her language, and I can tell

she's torn between being my surrogate parent and a fangirl. She's going to break soon. I know it. Auntsie powers up the stereo and places the album on the turntable. The crackling needle heightens our anticipation as we watch the record turn and wait for the opening guitar sounds.

"'Taxman,'" Auntsie announces. "Track four is one of my favorites. 'Here, There, and Everywhere.'"

Malcolm turns to me. "You should listen to that one. It's got that steady, in-the-pocket, understated Ringo drumming." Then he turns back to Auntsie. "I kinda dig the last track."

I'm wondering what the last track is when Auntsie reads it off the jacket.

"'Tomorrow Never Knows.'"

Mutual understanding then awkward silence passes between us. Auntsie's icy exterior begins to thaw.

"Let's eat. Your sister and Kate said they'll be back in time for dessert."

I'm sure they will. Evie's not going to miss an opportunity to spy for Mom.

I turn to Malcolm and explain. "My sister and her friend are here until Wednesday. They've been soaking up the sun like solar panels since yesterday morning."

"I'm more of a nighttime person," Malcolm says.

"Me too." Auntsie motions to the tats on her arms. "If I don't wear a long-sleeved swim shirt and SPF one hundred, these fade."

Malcolm takes a step closer and nods approvingly. "I like the Celtic knotwork design. I've always wanted to get a cross like that on my back."

"I know an excellent artist if you ever decide to do it. There's a six-month waiting list for her, but she's worth it."

Yep. Auntsie is definitely opening up.

Once we're seated around the small kitchen table, Auntsie asks Malcolm more questions than that guy with the swoopy hair from World News Tonight. I twirl my linguine around my fork and watch the volley between them.

Where is the rehearsal space?

Across the bridge.

Recording studio?

Atlantic Trax in Asbury Park.

Fancy.

Yeah. Last time my label paid.

Did you hire a producer?

Ricky Keyes.

Auntsie drops her fork. "Holy shit, are you kidding me? Ricky Keyes?!"

"Yep." Malcolm looks pleased. Hard to tell if it's because he hired this Ricky person or because Auntsie knows who he is. I'm not sure who to be impressed with. "He's coming up from Nashville. We only have him for seventy-two hours though, one long weekend. So we'll need to be efficient."

Auntsie turns to me and clears up my confusion.

"I interviewed Ricky back in the day. He was with a band called Amethyst. They had one radio hit. When the band broke up, he went solo, but he also went on to write and produce songs for big names like Weezer, Pink, Keith Urban, Katy Perry. He's a big deal."

Wow. Who knew my aunt was Ricky Keyes's biggest fan?

She turns toward Malcolm. "How on earth did you get him?"

"Friend of a friend. Ricky is doing me a huge favor. Having him onboard means everything. I know this demo will turn out awesome."

"What do you plan to do with the demo when you're finished?" she asks.

"Have copies pressed."

"CDs or vinyl?" Auntsie asks.

"Both. I want to sell copies at my merch table. I'm lining up a solo tour for the fall," he says.

"A solo tour? Where?" I blurt out. The thought of him leaving suddenly makes me nervous.

I caught him as he was taking a bite of Italian bread, so I have to wait for him to chew and sip his water before I get an answer.

"College towns between here and Florida. It's the tour I never…" He clears his throat and focuses on his bowl of linguine. "Yeah, so anyway, I also want to send a copy to this A&R guy I'm still in touch with. Try to get my label interested in me again. He says if he likes what he hears, he'll send someone out to our Labor Day weekend showcase at Keegan's. Even if it is in *Jersey*."

Auntsie shakes her head. "New York music snobs. Typical."

My palms start to sweat. "What's an A and R guy?"

"A&R stands for artists and repertoire—they're like talent scouts for record labels," Auntsie explains.

I look at Malcolm. "Are you sure you want me as your drummer? You should get someone better."

Malcolm clears his throat. "When I started my band, Gatsby, I was the only one who had any chops when it came to playing an instrument. The rest of those guys? They had some work to do. But the vibe felt right between us, ya know? Same thing this time around. It's about the vibe, and I have a good feeling about our power trio."

"But I'm going to make mistakes."

Malcolm waves away my protest.

"Trust me, it's going to be all right. Producers like Ricky can work miracles in the studio, and we still have plenty of time before the gig. If we need to, we can make it an acoustic set at Keegan's, and you can play percussion."

Auntsie chimes in. "I've always wanted to play tambourine in a band. Either that or the cowbell. How cool would that be?"

"If you're not a cow? Not very," I say.

"Oh, come on. It would be awesome," Auntsie says.

"Is that a hint?" Malcolm asks.

"Maybe." Auntsie winks. Anyone else would have let it go, but Auntsie?

Malcolm laughs. "It just so happens, I have a cowbell in my truck."

"Get out! Don't sit there. Finish your linguine, and bring it in."

I'm pretty sure this thing with Malcolm is happening.

FOURTEEN

After dinner, Auntsie holds the door open as Malcolm and I carry in the drums. She tells him to set up the equipment in the living room.

"Are you sure, Auntsie? They're going to take up a lot of space," I say.

"And they're loud," Malcolm offers.

"Yeah, I'm sure. Makes up for the baby toys and portable cribs I missed out on." She laughs, but there's a wistfulness behind her smile.

Malcolm moves quickly and methodically, setting up the kick drum and pedal, the snare, three toms, the hi-hat, and crash cymbals. He even brought a drum mat to put them on and his own sticks.

I stand back and stare at the finished product, like there's a bison in the middle of the living room.

"This is too much drum for me," I say.

Malcolm stands beside me and strokes his bearded chin.

"Probably. Ignore the toms and crash cymbals for now. Concentrate on the kick, the snare, and the hi-hat. Let me show you a basic groove."

He sits down behind the drums and starts tapping the hi-hat with one stick.

"These are your eighth notes," he says. "One and two and three and four and…add in the snare on the two and the four, like this, and the kick drum—"

"On the one and the three," I finish for him. You don't spend four years in the drumline without understanding the role of each drum and drummer.

"Right. I'm sure you've internalized all this. You know more than you think you know. You just have to get used to doing all three at once. This groove is perfect practice. It's hi-hat bass, hi-hat. Hi-hat snare, hi-hat. Just practice this over and over again with a metronome, keeping your tempo as even as possible."

It's not a totally foreign concept. I've already played combinations like this on my electronic drums, but I'm itching to try out the kit. Auntsie and I watch Malcolm keep an even, steady beat, and I repeat the rhythm in my head. *Hi-hat bass, hi-hat. Hi-hat snare, hi-hat.* Cymbals-drum, cymbals. Cymbals-drum, cymbals. Eventually Malcolm breaks away from the simplistic rhythm and gets fancy, throwing in fills using the toms and crash cymbals, speeding up his tempo and hitting harder before bringing it back down to the basic groove.

"Show off," I tease when he finally stops and stands up.

"Can't help it."

"I still say you should record your own drum parts."

He shakes his head.

"Unlike Prince, I'm not a perfectionist and I don't do 'alone.' I want to be in the studio with a band. End of story." He hands off his sticks to me like the baton in a relay. "Let's see what you've got."

The drumsticks are warm from his touch. I sit behind the kit and adjust the stool to my height. Before allowing myself to test the limits of my coordination and screw up in front of an audience, I launch into a marching band rhythm on only the snare before segueing into the part from "Sunday Bloody Sunday," the U2 song Malcolm told me to learn. I know I'm the one showing off now, and I keep expecting Malcolm or Auntsie to call me on it, but I can't stop myself. It's been too long since I've played a real snare, and before I know it, I'm taking it to the next level, performing one of the more mind-boggling solos in my repertoire. My hands snap up and down without me having to tell them what to do until finally, I wrap it up with a superfast roll and rim shot.

Auntsie starts clapping. "Quinn, baby. I didn't know you could that."

Malcolm smiles. "I kinda did."

One corner of my mouth turns up. "Don't be too impressed. I'm going to suck at the rhythm you just showed me."

"Don't overthink it."

I touch one stick to the hi-hat cymbals, press the pedal to open them a bit, and begin tapping out the eighth notes while counting in my head. *One and two and three and four and...* When I feel comfortable, I close my eyes and add in the snare. *Hi-hat snare, hi-hat. Hi-hat snare, hi-hat.*

"That's it, nice and steady," Malcolm encourages. "Now see if you can drop that bass on the one and the three."

I fail at my first few attempts as I try to get used to three different body parts moving independently of each other. Malcolm made it look easy. I struggle, trying to force my body to execute the rhythm in my head.

Eventually, I do what he said. I don't overthink. I don't think at all. I stop worrying about whether or not the water is cold and dive in. My stomach flutters like I've found my next crush as my mind and body fall into this basic groove.

"Right on," Malcolm says after a few minutes of watching me master it. "You're ready to play 'Back in Black.'"

"What? No way."

"Yes, way. That's the groove right there minus some fills."

"Ohh, I'm so putting it on!" Auntsie says.

"You're so not," I say, craning my neck toward her and throwing off my timing with my panic.

Too late. Auntsie's already retrieving the AC/DC album from the "A" section of her collection and dropping the needle on the record. Much to my horror, Auntsie begins singing the guitar intro while playing air guitar, and before I can accurately calculate this moment's mortification level, Malcolm chimes in with the opening lyrics, using his best, raspy metal voice.

I assume the karaoke routine is over after the intro, but apparently Malcolm and Auntsie are just getting started. They plow into the next verse with Malcolm on vocals and Auntsie on "guitar." I try to keep the beat steady, but it's nearly impossible to concentrate. It gets worse. I watch them exchange a knowing look, one that must give my aunt permission to launch into an air guitar solo, because that's exactly what she does.

Oh. My. God. I nearly drop both sticks.

I close my eyes and focus on the beat. When it's time for the next verse, Malcolm and Auntsie sing it together. It's so absurd that I start to giggle, which is also absurd because I'm so not a giggler. By the time the song reaches its climax, when the word "Baacck" gets repeated over and over, my need to join the fun outweighs any inhibitions or negative feelings I have about absurdity. I start singing with them and improv this crazy fill with crashing cymbals and a series of rolls that are totally out of time and don't come close to fitting the song, but I don't care. My arms are flailing like Animal from the Muppets, and I'm laughing so hard I'm afraid I might pee my pants.

Of course it's at that exact moment my sister and Kate walk in.

FIFTEEN

"We could hear you all the way up the block!"
my sister proclaims. "The neighbors across the street are on their
front porch. Do you know what they must be thinking?"

"That I've quit my job to become an air guitarist and backing
vocalist in a rock band?" Auntsie says.

The three of us start to laugh. Evie *tssks*. Her already pinkish
skin reddens. She hates to be teased.

"It's not funny."

She crosses her arms and stares at us. Auntsie snorts. I bite
my lower lip to stop myself from laughing. I wonder if Evie knows
she's turned into our mother.

"Evie, Kate, this is Malcolm," I say.

Malcolm shakes Kate's hand first. "Nice to meet you."

Evie's determined to stay angry, but Malcolm smoothly takes her hand in both of his, offering a sweet smile and extended eye contact, which coaxes a half grin out of my sister. Once a front man, always a front man. Not even Evie is immune to rock-star charm.

"Sorry if we upset the neighbors. After today we'll be moving to a rehearsal space."

Evie looks from Malcolm to Auntsie. "Wait. Did you really quit your job to join the band too?"

Poor Evie. It's hard to be so literal. Her IQ approaches genius level, but she doesn't always recognize a joke when she hears one.

"Yes, and to supplement my income, I'm going to be doing some runway modeling," Auntsie says.

I jump in. "No one quit their job, Evie. And by 'we,' Malcolm meant me and him."

"Although your aunt may sit in on cowbell or tambourine." Malcolm winks.

Auntsie gets excited. "That's right! Didn't you say you had that cowbell in your truck?"

Evie looks at me. "Did she have too much wine with dinner?"

"No, she's right. I *do* have a cowbell in my truck." Malcolm looks at me. "Want to come out with me to get it? I think I'm going to take off soon."

My eyes thank Malcolm for opening an escape hatch. I stand up from behind the drums and walk toward the door.

Malcolm approaches my aunt with an outstretched hand. "Thank you for dinner."

Auntsie grabs his hand and pulls him into a hug. "Any time. Thanks for the album."

"It was nothing," Malcolm says. But we all know it was more.

"Be right back," I say.

Auntsie waves her phone at me. "Go! I'm going to research classic rock songs that feature a cowbell while you're gone."

I'm pretty sure she's serious.

Outside, our feet crunch on the sand and pebble "lawn" as I follow Malcolm to the curb, where he parked his truck. The air smells delicious, like charcoal and burgers.

"Ah, meat. My aunt's determined to make me a vegetarian like her."

Malcolm laughs. "We'll have to go for steak sandwiches. I know a place."

The idea of going someplace, alone, with Malcolm makes my stomach float toward my heart.

He reaches over the side of the flatbed and lifts a heavy-duty milk crate filled with percussion instruments—tambourines, wood blocks, and a cowbell.

"Please do not tell my aunt."

"About us going out for meat?"

"About the contents of this box. One cowbell is quite

enough. If fact, maybe we leave that right here too. I'll tell her you made a mistake."

Malcolm puts the crate back in his truck and presses the cowbell into my hands. "No way. You saw how excited she was about finding that list."

He's right. I can't go back inside empty-handed. Malcolm places his hands on my shoulders and leans closer. Our eyes meet and we start talking at the same time.

"So, did I pass your aunt's test?" he asks.

"You're leaving in September?" I say.

We both say "Yeah" at the same time.

"Good, great!" Malcolm says in response to my "yeah."

Not good, not great, I want to say in response to his. I know we agreed this arrangement would be about recording Malcolm's demo and playing one gig, but what about when summer ends?

"How long will you be on the road?"

Malcolm's hands drop from my shoulders and he leans back against the truck.

"Depends on how many club dates I can book, but I'd like to make it to Gainesville and back by Thanksgiving." He scrunches his brow. "Guess you'll be long gone by then."

Will I? Malcolm has the next few months mapped out, and I'm still stalled on the side of the road. Both thoughts— Malcolm's plan and my lack thereof—make me tired.

"I honestly have no idea where I'll be or what I'll be doing this fall. I want to keep living here with my aunt but my mother will never go for it if I don't have a solid life plan. Every time I think about it, I get overwhelmed."

Malcolm squeezes my hand and looks me in the eye. "Do what I do then. Think about one day at a time."

I look up at him. "Okay. I pick…Thursday." The night of our first band practice.

Malcolm laughs. "Thursday is solid day. It has a lot going for it as days go."

Impulse overtakes me and I lean up and kiss his cheek.

"I thought you weren't supposed to kiss me?"

I step back and give him a half smile. "You weren't supposed to kiss *me*."

He shakes his head and opens the truck door. "Thursday," he says with conviction.

"Thursday," I repeat.

Of course, I can't think about Thursday without thinking about Wednesday, when Mom arrives and I have to tell her about the band. But right now, I don't want to think about that either. I've got a lot of work to do, and I'm anxious to log as many practice hours as possible on those drums.

SIXTEEN

"So let me get this straight," Mom says. She's buzzing around Auntsie's living room like a wasp on steroids, casting dirty looks at my drum kit. I long to be behind it, practicing until my arms ache like they have for the past three days. Instead, I'm being subjected to one of Mom's infamous tirades.

And she's only getting started.

"I send her to live with you this summer so she can get her head on straight, and you let her join a band?"

I wince, closing my blue eye—my dad's eye. The bad one, as I've come to think of it. Mom and Evie are both brown-eyed.

"It's a *band*, not a satanic cult, Gemma," Auntsie says.

"A band you let her join!" Mom volleys back.

Oh boy. I hunch over in my seat. I've got at least four

inches on Mom, but when she gets like this, I try to make myself smaller. Not that it matters. Mom and my aunt act like me, Evie, and Kate (poor Kate!) aren't even here—like I'm not almost nineteen and legally able to make my own decisions.

"I didn't let her do anything. I told her you had the final say. I did the initial vetting."

Mom came straight from work dressed in a pantsuit and looking very lawyerly. She stops her incessant pacing and glares at Auntsie.

"And?"

"He seems like a good guy. Plus, she's not joining a band per se. It's temporary. A few practices, one recording session, and a gig. He leaves in September," Auntsie says.

"Leaves?"

I clear my throat. "He's doing a solo tour of college towns between here and Florida. It's the tour he and his band never got to take."

Mom looks at Auntsie. "Hmph. Sounds familiar. Because they broke up?"

"Because they died," Auntsie answers for me.

Mom looks at me, really looks at me, for the first time since she arrived twenty minutes ago. That's when she told me I look terrible in Grammy's glasses. Now she looks ready to pounce.

"How?" she asks.

"They were in a tour van accident. The drummer and guitarist were killed. The bassist moved to Georgia," I explain.

Mom crosses her arms. "Were drugs or alcohol involved?"

I shake my head. *No, your honor, they were not.*

"They were hit by a semi. The driver fell asleep and slammed into them. Pushed their van off the road."

"That's horrible. I can't imagine."

Like a hot air balloon coming to rest, Mom eases herself between Auntsie and I on the couch. Her flowery perfume wafts my way, tickling my nose. She always wears too much. It's not enough that I can always feel Mom's presence—I have to smell it too.

"It is horrible. It took Malcolm two years to write new songs and attempt a comeback. He asked this guy Liam I work with to play guitar on his CD. Malcolm's gonna play bass. He's mostly a singer and songwriter, but he plays like every instrument."

"What about your life plan, Quinn? All I'm hearing about is Malcolm, not you. How does his grand *comeback* fit into your plan?" Mom air quotes "comeback," which is both dated and annoying. I cross my arms over my chest and try to come up with an acceptable answer.

My silence agitates Mom.

She continues, "You know what? If that question is too hard, maybe it's time for you to come home. I'm beginning to think this whole arrangement was a mistake."

"Wasn't the goal of this 'whole arrangement' to give Quinn time to figure things out by herself?" Auntsie tries to help but winds up poking the hornet's nest.

"What do you know about what Quinn needs? You're her aunt, not her mother."

Auntsie looks stung. "I know I'm not a mom."

Now I'm the one who's pissed. "She acts like a mom though," I say. "Auntsie waits up for me when I work late. Makes me coffee and home-cooked meals. Takes me with her to volunteer at the animal shelter. You don't have to be a mom to care about someone."

"Thanks, Quinn baby," Auntsie says softly.

Mom straightens her shoulders. "Give me one good reason I should let you join this band."

The answer comes, quite unexpectedly, from Evie. "Because he makes her laugh."

"What?" Mom and Auntsie say at the same time.

"He makes her laugh. Not just smile, but belly laugh. I don't remember the last time I heard Quinn laugh that way."

Tears prick my eyes. Is that true?

With Lynn, I laughed all the time. She had this completely infectious giggle and once we got started, we didn't stop until we were holding our stomachs and gasping for air. Half the time, we had no idea what we were laughing about. It's been three years, and I'm still discovering the parts of me that died with my best friend. There are a lot of really terrible things about losing a friend, but one of the worst is how they take pieces of you with them. No one talks about that though, because it would make you seem like a selfish asshole on account of you're still breathing and they're not.

The room falls silent, and I stare at my feet. Finally Mom speaks.

"You can't forget to focus on you. To give some thought, real thought, to what you want."

I look up hopefully. "So I can do it?" Evie and I exchange a glance that says: *Thank you, little sis. Anytime, big sis.*

Then I turn back at Mom. For a moment, I think she's going to hug me. And for a moment, I really want her to hug me. But she stands abruptly.

"On two conditions. One, you cannot get involved with this boy romantically. Rockers make bad boyfriends. And two, when summer ends, so does your stint in the band." She points a finger at me. "Come September, don't let me hear that you're packing your bags and going on tour."

Or what?! I want to say, but I'm mostly getting what I want, so I keep my mouth shut. That's why I'm surprised when Auntsie pipes up.

"Like that would be so bad? Dating a musician and going on tour?"

"I don't know, Annie. You tell me. Would it?" What's Auntsie thinking? We just calmed the angry hornet. And what is Mom talking about?

"I want more for Quinn too," Auntsie concedes.

"Good," Mom says. "Then we're all on the same page."

I don't know about the same page, or even the same book. Same library, maybe. But the glacier that's been keeping Mom and I apart? It may have begun to thaw. I can't wait to tell Malcolm I'll be at rehearsal on Thursday.

SEVENTEEN

The rehearsal space turns out to be a house—a palatial house on the opposite side of the bay from where Auntsie lives.

"Holy fucking McMansion," Liam says when we pull up. He offered to give me a ride when I complained how the drums Malcolm loaned me wouldn't fit in my car. Liam drives his dad's old Cherokee.

"Looks like it's for sale," I say, nodding toward the sign.

I get out of Liam's Jeep and walk around back to start loading in. Malcolm says it's important to get used to hauling and setting up my own kit. I don't see why. The studio where we're going to be recording in two weeks has a sweet set of drums for me to use, and we're only doing one gig. Plus, Mom made it pretty clear that my time in a rock band comes with an expiration date. If Malcolm ever becomes famous, I'll be like Pete Best, the first Beatles drummer who faded into obscurity. Not Ringo Starr.

Malcolm's smiling and holding the door for us as I lug the bass drum up the pink brick walkway and maneuver sideways and awkwardly over the threshold.

"Nice house," I say, trying not to sound as out of breath as I am. The open floor plan features slate gray hardwood floors, high ceilings, and bay views from every window. It's pretty, but it lacks hominess and charm.

"My parents own it."

"They're here?" I wasn't expecting to meet them tonight.

He shakes his head. "They're flipping it. My mom's a real estate agent and my dad's a contractor." He opens his arms and gestures around the house. "And this? This is the glue that keeps them together. They're letting me stay here until it's sold."

"Sweet," Liam says as he offers his hand in some kind of bro shake, fist-bump combo.

I put down my drum and walk into the kitchen to the sliding glass doors, which lead out to a deck and in-ground pool.

"Let me open that," Malcolm says. He reaches around me to unlock the door, brushing my hip and making my heart double pump. I hadn't realized he was behind me. I step out onto the deck. The air smells like summer—fresh-cut grass, chlorine, and…

"Mmm, honeysuckle," I say out loud.

"It runs the length of the property."

"Best smell ever." Ever since Lynn's funeral, I've preferred fragrant living flowers to dead floral arrangements. Good thing I've never had to worry about a boyfriend sending me bouquets for Valentine's Day or my birthday.

I walk to the far side of the deck, where I can look beyond the pool and small lawn to the dock and Barnegat Bay. I can see the water tower near Auntsie's house and know exactly where I am. With a high-powered telescope, I might be able to see into my bedroom window from here.

Malcolm leans on the deck rail beside me.

"We're at about the same latitude."

"I was thinking the same thing." I can watch the sunset over the water from Auntsie's house. Malcolm can watch it rise.

Liam joins us and nudges my shoulder. "By boat we could be here in ten minutes, Q. Hey, maybe next time we borrow the Clark's Bayliner!" I hear about Andrew's parents almost as much as I hear about Andrew.

"And load my drums on and off the boat? I'll pass." I flick a thumb over my shoulder. "I'm going to head out to the Jeep and get my toms and cymbals."

Liam begins to walk away. "Let me get my amp out first, Q."

I turn to follow Liam, and Malcolm lightly touches my elbow.

"Q? That's awfully cute."

His expression tells me I should set him straight.

"It beats 'Benny,' which is what he used to call me, or 'Quinny.' That's what his girlfriend, Kiki, calls me. Know what the funny thing is?"

"What's that?"

"I still like Cat's Eye best."

I smile, and Malcolm's face relaxes.

"Q! Hurry up!" Liam yells from inside. He's been evolving from douchebag to impatient child. He continues to scream. "Get your shit and bring it in! We don't have all night!" Of course evolution takes time.

"I better finish loading in."

"I'll help."

"No, no. If I'm going to be a drummer, I've got to act like one."

"Let's start with the covers," Malcolm says when we're all set up. "How about we do 'Seven Nation Army' first. Ready?"

Liam nods.

"Quinn, count us in," Malcolm says.

With sweaty hands, I clack my sticks four times, nearly

dropping one. How embarrassing. I've been practicing in front of a full-length mirror all week, assessing and correcting the strange facial tics I've developed while trying to keep time and make sure my boobs don't shake too much. I've resorted to lightly biting my lower lip to deal with the former problem, and a double layer of sports bras for the latter. I didn't anticipate needing gymnastics chalk for my sticky palms.

Luckily the song begins with two measures of bass, giving me time to wipe my hands on my thighs before chiming in with the floor tom. That's the second biggest drum with a sound not quite as low as the bass. It's all me and Malcolm in the beginning. Bass and drum. No guitar part yet. In my head, I know my kick drum and his bass need to lock in on the fourth count, but it's hard to do while keeping the beats on the hi-hat and the tom even and steady. Liam joins in with guitar on the chorus and bridge and then it's back to bass and guitar.

Our first run through is a mess, on my part at least. It's a simple enough song, but I'm fucking it up. I lose time whenever I try to get fancy. Malcolm starts off patient, locking eyes with me and nodding in time to help us get tight musically. But I keep getting overwhelmed, and he's losing patience. I can tell.

"I need a cigarette," he mutters after our fourth attempt at the song.

This is it, I'm thinking. I'm out of the band. Goodbye Pete Best, hello Ringo.

Liam offers me a sympathetic look as Malcolm walks out of the garage and into the attached kitchen.

"You're trying too hard, Q. You can do this."

"I thought I could," I mutter. I was so much better practicing at home.

"Play the snare part for 'Sunday Bloody Sunday.' Warm up while Malcolm cools off."

I could easily play that part. But Malcolm's heard me do it before. He won't be impressed, and I won't redeem myself.

"Liam? Can you play the guitar part for the third track on Malcolm's demo?"

Malcolm needs to come up with some names for these songs.

"You mean the one that begins like this?"

Liam plays the opening riff.

"Yes, that's it. Keep going."

I pick up my sticks and start playing the drum part I've been working out at home—the same part that played in my head the first time I heard the song.

Liam's smile tells me we sound good. By the time we reach the chorus a second time, Malcolm's back. Wordlessly, he lifts his bass from its stand and starts playing. The warm mellow *bum, bum, bum* mixes with Liam's lead guitar and my simple but effective drumming. I make it to the end without losing time once.

Malcolm's not exactly smiling, but he's not pissed anymore either.

"Again."

We play it twice more before Malcolm asks, "Which other songs do you have drum parts for?"

"All of them, except 'That Last Night.'" I don't want to tell him that ever since my freak-out at Keegan's, it's been hard for me to listen to that song.

We work our way through three of Malcolm's originals, stopping and starting when Malcolm wants to change something or tweak the bass and drum parts. To his credit, Liam nails every guitar part, every time. He's really good.

When we're finished, we sit around eating Sun Chips and drinking iced tea. Malcolm offered us beer, but we both declined. I'm wondering why he keeps alcohol in the house at all. Is that wise? Is it allowed? I need to get my hands on the NA rule book. I don't want to invade Malcolm's privacy about rehab, but I need to know more.

Malcolm claps his hands and rubs them together like he's warming them over a fire.

"So, when are we going to do this again? Tomorrow?"

"Liam and I are working," I say. "Saturday?"

"Can't. I'm going to a wedding with Kiki," says Liam.

"Whose?" I ask.

"First cousin, family friend? Don't know. She told me, but I stopped listening after 'wedding.'"

"How about Sunday night?" Malcolm suggests.

"Works for me," I say. I'll have time to go to the shelter and hang out with Auntsie beforehand.

"Sunday night sounds perfect," Liam says. "I'm going to need some me time after spending the day in a suit doing the chicken dance." He unplugs his guitar and winds his chord.

"Leave your amp, if you want," Malcolm says. He turns to me. "You can leave the drums too."

"But I'm going to want to practice."

"So practice here," Malcolm says.

"When?" What happened to rocker boot camp and learning to haul my own gear?

Malcolm shrugs. "Whenever."

"Uh, okay."

Malcolm walks toward the wall to smack the garage door opener.

"Here, I'll give you the security code for the keypad so you can practice whenever you want. I don't have to be here."

Liam grins and waggles his eyebrows as he steps under the still-opening garage door. I shoot him a look that screams *quit it*, but I can tell he's smiling like a cat with a canary in its mouth as he walks down the driveway to his Jeep.

"I knew it," Malcolm says as we step, side by side, into a wall of humid air. The crickets are chirping and the streetlights cast a yellow glow over everything.

ALAMEDA FREE LIBRARY

"Knew what?" I'm still distracted by Liam, who keeps tossing glances over his shoulder.

"That this was the right band for my songs. Not the right one for a White Stripes tribute band maybe, but the right band for my songs."

He walks me toward the car. The flowers lining the driveway and lawn remind me of summer nights back home. Simpler summers, before life got so fucked up. I smile and breathe deep. I practiced so, so hard this week, working on my rudiments and trying to get those drum parts down. I'm enjoying the unfamiliar sensation of doing something right.

Malcolm closes the gap between us. Our shoulders touch, and he brushes my fingertips with his.

"What are you doing tomorrow before work?" he asks.

"Practicing here," I say without hesitation.

He squeezes my hand and smiles. "Right answer."

We both know I wouldn't be able to stay away.

EIGHTEEN

I punch in the four-digit code Malcolm gave me, and the garage door rises. *This is too weird*, a tiny voice echoes from some deep brain canyon. Not because I'm here without Malcolm. He told me he'd be at the gas station when I arrived and that I should let myself in. But because he gave me access to this house, his space... There's an intimacy there, right? I'm not saying it's the romantic kind. But it's the kind of closeness I've been without for a while now. The kind I'm not really sure I deserve.

I glance both ways over my shoulders before stepping into the garage. Two girls on beach cruisers pedal down the street. The one on the purple bike rings her bell, and the other turns her helmeted head toward me and grins. She's at the awkward age where her grown-up teeth look too big for her mouth. I smile back, or at least I think I do—I'm hit so hard with a memory of who I used to be that it's hard to tell. *Lynn, watch this, no hands! Come on, pedal faster, we got this!*

Somewhat lightheaded, I step inside the mostly empty garage and walk past my drums toward the kitchen door where the garage controls are. With a shaky hand, I slam the button and watch the shadow descend as the door closes behind me. I take a deep breath and put down my drawstring tote and plastic Wawa bag with salty snacks and iced tea on an empty workbench. I move toward my drums, anxious to pound away the cocktail of weirdness and melancholy churning in my gut.

There's a note taped to the hi-hat.

Open the kitchen door to let in the AC. It gets hot in here.—M

It's a cloudy day and already close to four, so despite the full-body flush brought on by my brief encounter with my former self, the garage is cool and comfortable. That may change after I've been playing for a while, but I need to break through the nagging feeling that I shouldn't be here. *Here* being more than this garage.

I pull my sticks from my back pocket and run through some warm-ups before putting in my earbuds and cueing up Malcolm's songs. I don't waste any time. Malcolm said he'd be home after five, and I have to be at Keegan's by seven.

I close my eyes and let the melodies and rhythms pour into

me like hot wax. The songs become part of me, and I lose all sense of time and place, pausing only long enough to stretch my cramping fingers. I practice the drum part for each track over and over again and don't move on to the next until I'm certain I've got it right. When I reach the last track, the song I can't bring myself to write a drum part for, I skip it and start back at the beginning.

After more than an hour, thirst and hunger finally get the better of me. My iced tea and Fritos call from inside the Wawa bag. When I lay my drumsticks on my snare and pull out my earbuds, it's like I'm emerging from swimming underwater. I blink my eyes.

Malcolm is standing in the kitchen doorway. "Hey."

"Hey." I look down, suddenly self-conscious about the skimpy tank top I'm wearing, the sweat dripping down my chest, and my glasses that are forever sliding down my nose.

Malcolm holds up a white paper bag and grins. "I brought meat."

He's wearing dark gray work pants and a light gray tee with the Kwik Fill logo where the designer's mark would be on fancier shirts. He looks better than any country club guy, if you ask me.

"I'm dripping with sweat," I say. Ugh! When am I going to realize that sometimes it's better to say nothing?

His brow furrows with concern. "You should have opened the kitchen door. I'll bet you didn't bring a bikini either."

Malcolm texted me earlier and said to bring a swimsuit. Specifically a *string* bikini. I walk toward him.

"I brought a perfectly acceptable one-piece."

"Your choice. You're gonna feel overdressed when I skinny-dip though."

The thought of Malcolm in the buff makes me blush all over, but I don't give him a chance to see he's rattled me.

"Ha, ha." I nudge past him into the cool kitchen. "Ahh, the air feels nice."

"The pool will feel even better. There's a bathroom in the foyer if you want to change."

I take a deep breath and inhale the aroma of peppers and onions.

"Mmm. Are those steak sandwiches?"

Malcolm nods.

"Okay if we eat, then swim?"

"I offer you my naked self and all you want is food?"

"I've already seen your naked self, and yes, I'm starving."

"Ouch."

"Nudity was not in the plan. Remember?"

"As per our agreement, you said I couldn't be naked in your bed, implying all other locations are fair game."

"Believe what you want. Can I have my sandwich now?"

We eat poolside, on a wrought iron table under an umbrella. Malcolm talks about the extensive renovation his parents did on the house in order to flip it. Music plays through the fake rocks that house the outdoor sound system, and the pool filter hums.

"I feel like I'm at a fancy resort. A resort that serves the best cheesesteaks I've ever eaten." I tilt my chin toward Malcolm. "Is there anything on my face?"

He smiles. "Besides cheese and ketchup, you mean? Come 'ere." He puts one hand on my forehead and licks his thumb like he's about to "mommy wash" my face.

I scooch back and laugh. "Don't you dare!"

He throws up his hands. "I tried. The pool water will have to take care of it. Ready to swim?"

I glance at my phone. I only have about forty-five minutes until I have to be at Keegan's, but if I French braid my wet hair I can make it.

"My stuff's still in the garage. I'll be right back."

"Go. I'll clean up."

While I'm in the garage gathering my bags, I hear Malcolm in the kitchen crumpling our trash and opening and closing cabinets. It feels like we're playing house and I hate to admit it, but I like it. I put my drumsticks in my drawstring tote and I'm about to go back inside, when the garage door starts to open. At first I think I hit some switch accidentally or that Malcolm triggered it from inside so he can take out the trash. But as the door opens, I see pink polished toes in high-heeled sandals, long tanned legs, a Lycra miniskirt, and the face of a curly-haired girl who looks as surprised to see me as I am to see her.

"Heeey!" she says too loudly and cheerily. "Is Malcolm here?"

Malcolm appears in the kitchen doorway in a flash. Either he heard the garage door open or Miss Lycra's peppy voice. My heart yammers as he approaches, and the nervous look he shoots me when she throws her arms around him in a too-tight embrace does nothing to calm me down.

"Tamara, hey," Malcolm says as he peels her off him. "This is Quinn. She's my—"

He hesitates, and I bail him out.

"His drummer. I'm his drummer. We were wrapping up a rehearsal." I jut out my hand in a clumsy, and perhaps slightly aggressive, way that startles her.

When she recovers, she takes my hand.

"Nice to meet you." she says.

"Same," I say. I look back and forth between Malcolm and Tamara, trying to guess their story. But since I already know the part where she has the code to his garage, do I really need to know more? No. I don't. I sling my bag over my shoulder and grab my untouched snacks.

"I should go. I don't want to be late for work." Then I walk away as quickly as I can without running down the driveway and don't stop until I get to my car.

"Quinn, wait!" I hear Malcolm call as I slam the door shut. I watch him in the rearview mirror, jogging toward me.

I lock the doors and turn the key, but of course my car chooses this exact moment to stall. Malcolm is beside my car now, banging on my window. I twist the key a second time and the engine turns over, but I can't drive away. Not with all these thoughts percolating like Pop Rocks in my brain. I can't let this moment become any more awkward than it already is.

As soon as I roll down the window, Malcolm takes a step back, runs a hand through his hair, and begins talking in a rush.

"Back there, it isn't what you think. I can explain."

I force a smile. "There's nothing to explain, really. It's... I gotta get to work. Thanks for the cheesesteaks. See you at practice on Sunday."

Before Malcolm can say another word, I drive away slowly, carefully, acutely aware that there are kids around here who play ball in the streets and cruise around on bikes and may not always pay attention to oncoming traffic.

NINETEEN

"What's up with you tonight, Q? You're acting weirder than usual, and that's saying a lot."

Liam's right. I'm flustered but still trying to pay attention. We stand behind the sound board as the first band sound checks and Liam explains how to mic the instruments and get all the levels right. He thought it would be a good idea for me to learn in case there's ever an emergency and I have to fill in. I'm honored that he trusts me enough to let me encroach on his turf. Maybe that's why I open up unexpectedly.

"I had a strange practice over at Malcolm's place today."

He looks at me, concerned.

"Strange how?" I open my mouth to answer as the guitarist cranks out a loud rift. Liam puts up one finger. "Hold that thought." He moves some levers on the board. "I'm adjusting the levels. Turning down the guitar and boosting the bass," he explains. Then he turns toward the band. "Try that again, guitar and bass together."

The band complies. The guitarist doesn't look happy.

"I need a little more of me and less of him," he says, nodding to the bassist.

"Oh, of course he does," Liam mumbles. "He's wrong, but I'll give him what he wants for now." Then he tells the band to run through a song. He turns to me when they start to play. "Back to the strangeness at Malcolm's. You didn't have sex, did you?"

My cheeks turn instantly red. "God, Liam, no. What would make you say something like that?"

"Oh, I dunno, maybe the palpable sexual tension every time you two are together. I mean, he gave you the code to his garage. *I* didn't get the code."

"It's for convenience. So I can play drums there whenever I want."

"Is that what they're calling it these days? Playing drums. I thought it was Netflix and chill. Who knew?" Liam shrugs and gives me that wry smile of his.

"Quit teasing," I say.

"Look, if you like him, go for it. Avoid all the angsty buildup." He's being serious.

"First, who says I even like him?"

Liam shoots me his *give me a break* face. I keep talking.

"Okay, so I like him, but that leads to my second point. Wouldn't that screw up the band? And third, I'm not the only girl with the code to Malcolm's garage."

Liam's riveted. "Really? No shit. Tell me everything."

We're interrupted by the guitarist. "Hey, can you double-check my vocal mic? I can't hear myself."

"Diva," Liam mumbles and moves a lever. "Sure! Try it now."

I lower my voice while the guitarist sings a few lines a cappella.

"She arrived in all her pink Lycra glory while I was there."

"What did Malcolm do?"

"Chased me to my car. He wanted to explain."

"Then you should let him. Look, I'm far from being an expert about this stuff, but I can tell you that last year I caused a misunderstanding between my sister and Connor. This was before he was her boyfriend, when she was still dating Andrew. I thought I was protecting her, but the situation snowballed, and in the end, I almost got her killed. As it is, she got in a bad car accident. I'm not proud of what I did, I feel guilty every day, but I learned that a lot of mistakes can be avoided by talking about stuff before things get away from you."

"Wow. What happened?"

"Connor and I got in a screaming match. Lucy got so pissed off at us both that she took off driving in a bad rainstorm. She was hit broadside in an intersection." Liam can't look at me. "It could have been so much worse. Thank God it wasn't. I don't know what I'd do without her."

Maybe Malcolm was right about the three of us having some kind of special chemistry. We should call our trio "Albatross" with all the proverbial guilt we have hanging around our necks.

My silence makes Liam nervous.

"What? You think I'm a jerk now. I shouldn't have told you," he says.

"Nope. I think you made me forget why I ever thought you were a douchebag."

"Wait, what? You thought I was a douchebag?"

"Don't worry. It didn't last long." I put my arm around him and give him a side squeeze. "Thank you."

"No problem. Hey, if things don't pan out with Malcolm, I'll introduce you to Andrew. I think you two would really hit it off." Again with Andrew. Liam puts his arm around my waist and returns my side hug as the band finishes their song.

"Uh, I hope we're not interrupting anything," the guitarist says into the mic.

"I was just thinking the same thing," says a voice behind me. Malcolm.

When I turn around, he's standing there looking equal parts angry and sad.

"Can we talk? Outside?"

When we push through the exit, Malcolm walks toward the back of the building, away from the streetlights and into the shadows of the alley behind the bar. When he stops to face me, I don't give him a chance to talk.

I take two steps forward to close the space between us. I put one hand on his shoulder and with the other, I reach up to caress his neck and jawline. His pupils widen and a question flashes in his eyes right before my lips touch his. It takes him a few seconds to return my kiss—I'm pretty sure I startled him—but when he does, he grabs my hips, pulls me close, and slips his hands into my back pockets. As our bodies collide, something better than goose bumps, or electricity, or butterflies passes between us. It's more like a click. The sound of puzzle pieces falling into place.

"I thought I wasn't allowed to kiss you?" he asks when we finally separate.

"I kissed you. You were kissing me back."

He puts his hands on my shoulders and touches my forehead with his.

"I have to say, when I walked in here tonight and saw you with Liam, well…this was the last thing I expected."

"Liam's totally in love with his girlfriend. He was giving me advice about you."

"Me?"

I nod. "I was kind of upset when I got here tonight."

"I figured. I know Tamara showing up like that looked bad,

but it's not what you think. She was someone I knew before rehab. Someone I hadn't treated very nicely. I was trying to make amends."

"By giving her the code to your garage?"

"I did that before I met you. I haven't seen her in weeks."

"Okay, I get it. I shouldn't have asked. It's none of my business."

"Look, I'm not going to say she and I never hung out. She used to get me scrips for pills. Her mother's a dentist and I don't know how she pulled it off... Anyway, I was more interested in the pills than her. That was when I was more interested in pills than anything or anyone around me. I did a lot of stuff I wasn't proud of, including stealing cash from my parents and crashing real estate open houses and searching peoples' medicine cabinets to get high."

"Why are you telling me all this?" I try to turn away from him, but he puts his hands on my shoulders and looks into my eyes.

"I'm telling you this because it's been a long time since I cared about what anyone else thought of me. What you think of me matters, Cat's Eye, and I want to be honest with you," he says. "The reason Tamara stopped by tonight was to give me these."

Malcolm reaches into his front pocket and pulls out a Ziploc bag with four oval white pills. The bag is snack size, the kind that should be holding Goldfish crackers or pretzels, not painkillers.

"Why would she give you this? She knows you're recovering, right? Why didn't you give them back?" The hairs on my neck prickle. Maybe I shouldn't have rushed into that kiss.

Malcolm closes his hand around the bag.

"I asked her for them a while ago. Before I met you, before I started writing songs again. I...I wanted a few around for an emergency. I would never take them, but somehow knowing that I could if I wanted to, made me feel better. On the way over here, I realized I'm not strong enough to keep these around. It would be like being on a diet and having a refrigerator stocked with all of my favorite junk foods. I know it's asking a lot, but would you hold them for me?"

I kind of knew what he was talking about. I carry a Xanax with me at all times, just in case. A lot of people with anxiety do the same thing. Knowing it's there calms me down, but taking them makes me feel weak. I explain this to Malcolm.

"So you get it?" he says. "Sort of?"

I nod. "But it's different for me. I take Xanax to stop panic attacks, not to get high. They give me such a killer headache when they wear off that I hate taking them. I've never been addicted to them or anything else."

He laces his fingers with mine and pulls me close. Until now, maybe.

"Well then, you're lucky."

Am I? I'm not so sure about that or anything else for

that matter. But Malcolm's lips touch mine again, and all thoughts, good or bad, dissipate like rain on the sidewalk on a hot summer day.

"So," he says. "You'll hold these for me?"

I open my hand, and he gives me the Ziploc bag. *It's just four pills*, I think as I shove them into my front pocket. So why do they feel so heavy?

TWENTY

Back inside, I seesaw between anticipation at seeing Malcolm again and worry that he's on the verge of doing something stupid. Malcolm's on his way to meet with his sponsor at an all-night diner, but I can't help thinking he shouldn't be alone tonight, or any night. How's he going to go on the road by himself this fall? Are there other Tamaras out there who can hook him up with painkillers? The inherent danger is right there in the name, isn't it? And yet, one good toothache can score you a prescription that could lead to an addiction.

Even with all these thoughts swirling in my brain, the rush from kissing Malcolm has yet to wear off, and I guess it shows.

"Hey, baby girl," Arnie says when I bring him his drink.

Being called *baby girl* by anybody else would be creepy,

but somehow, coming from Arnie, it's benign. Elmo really is an apropos nickname.

"What's going on, Arnie?"

"Other than breathing? Not much. Not much. But look at you. Your light is on tonight. You got a secret you're not telling us?"

"No secrets, Arnie. I'm an open book."

Arnie chuckles, but he's right. I do have secrets—about Lynn, about why I wear my bracelet, about what happened with my band teacher—and Malcolm is one of the few people who knows about more than one of those. Now Malcolm's secrets are becoming mine too. Maybe it's time to come clean with my aunt about his stint in rehab since it's clear his struggles aren't over and he's becoming more involved in my life.

I wait until my break, then step outside to call Auntsie.

"What's wrong?" she asks by way of greeting. This is what happens when you mostly communicate by text.

"Everything's fine. Malcolm's having a bad night, and I was thinking I should check on him after work."

"Bad night how?"

I planned to tell her about Malcolm being a recovering addict and the pills in my pocket. After all, that's why I called her. I *almost* tell her, but it's late, and it's complicated, and in the end, I chicken out. *I'll tell her eventually*, I promise myself. Because I know keeping something this huge from my aunt is wrong.

"He says he's been thinking about the accident a lot more

lately. He seems kind of sad and lonely. I think he could use some company tonight."

"And let me guess, that company is you?"

"I was thinking I should stop by after work."

"At one in the morning?" There's a long pause. "Quinn, baby. I worry about you driving around at all hours. I worry, period."

"I'll text when I get there and again on my way home."

Auntsie lets out a long breath. "Go. Text me."

"You're the best."

"Spare me the flattery and use a condom."

"Auntsie!"

"Kidding. No, I'm not. Be careful. If anything ever happened to you—"

"Auntsie, nothing's going to happen to me."

"Love you," she says.

"Love you too."

I text Malcolm before I go back inside Keegan's.

Can I stop by after work?

I'll leave the kitchen door open.

Our exchange gives me the peace of mind I need to get through the rest of my shift. On my way out the door, I tell Liam to have a good time at the wedding. He replies with a groan. "See you Sunday. Hope you get some *drum practice* in before then."

I throw a stray piece of Chex Mix at him, stick out my tongue, and head toward the door.

Malcolm's neighborhood is eerie quiet when I step out of my car. I look up and down the street, afraid I might hear the tinkling of girlish laugher or the sound of a bike bell. Was that only this morning?

I hustle up the driveway before my thoughts and imagination get away from me. I botch the garage door code on the first attempt and have to reenter it. Once inside, I walk/run to the kitchen door, which is wide open. The house, like the neighborhood, is too still, and the only light comes from the giant flat screen. I spot Malcolm, headphones on, sprawled on the oversized sofa in front of the television. He smiles and opens his arms when I step between him and the screen. I lay down beside him, and he puts his arm around me and kisses the top of my head.

"Whatcha watching?" I ask.

He pulls off the headphones and turns up the sound.

"*Pulp Fiction*. It's genius. Want me to start it from the beginning?"

"It's okay. I'll catch on."

I lay my head against his chest and listen to the soft *chuh, chuh, chuh* of his heart. He doesn't ask why I stopped by, or if I still have the pills he asked me to hold. I don't ask about his meeting with his sponsor or whether or not he can handle being on the road by himself this fall. We just stare in comfortable silence at the images on the screen until I start to doze off and he strokes the side of my face with his knuckles.

Dazed, I sit up and try to chase the sleep away. My heart thrums with fear. I was starting to fall into my familiar Lynn nightmare.

"Why don't you stay?" he asks.

"I told my aunt I'd be home. I have to be up early tomorrow for work."

"Call her. I'll make sure you're up."

I reach for my phone and suddenly remember that I was supposed to text when I got here.

"Shit." I whisper.

"Everything okay?"

"Yeah." I fire off a quick text to Auntsie.

Sorry!!! I forgot to text when I got here. Don't be mad. Is it okay if I stay over?

I wince when I send it. She texts back in seconds. Only because I don't want you driving. We'll talk tomorrow.

Then I lie back against Malcolm, my body relaxing as it was before.

I wake up when I hear the sliding glass door opening and squint to see Malcolm stepping onto the deck. I reach for my bedazzled vintage glasses on the coffee table, gather up the plush Mets blanket I'm wrapped in, and follow him. The bay, the treetops, and Malcolm all are shadowed against the pale orange light inching up the horizon. The deck is wet with dew and for a second, I think about retreating to get my shoes, but Malcolm looks over his shoulder and sees me.

"Hey." His voice is gravelly.

I step beside him.

"Hey. What are you doing up at way-too-early o'clock?"

"I like watching the sunrise, knowing I made it through one more day. It's a habit that started when I had to give up the old one. That and smoking."

"Did you sleep at all?"

One corner of his mouth turns up. "Better than I usually do. I'm a bit of an insomniac."

"Guess I must be the cure for insomnia. It's either me or this fuzzy blanket. Or the combination."

Malcolm puts his arm around me and I stop babbling. He laughs a little to himself.

"What?"

"Quinn in a blanket," he jokes.

I bump his hip with mine. "Hey! It's no joke. I'm replacing Tylenol PM."

He laughs again. "Where did you come from Cat's Eye?" he says, pushing my glasses up on my nose.

After that, neither of us says anything as we watch the golden sun lift the shade on the darkness as it climbs higher into the sky.

"You know the sunrise is only an illusion," Malcolm says. "Atmospheric refraction makes it look like we're seeing the sun when it's actually still below the horizon for about another eight minutes."

I look at him and raise my eyebrows.

"What? It's true. I saw it on *Cosmos*. Insomniacs watch a lot of TV. And read a lot of books."

"That reminds me, I loved the book you gave me."

"It's one of my favorites."

"I keep forgetting to give it back to you."

"Keep it. It was meant to be a gift."

"Thank you."

We should be talking about more than optical illusions and gifted books. I wrack my brain for the right way to bring up the pills he asked me to hold, the reason I wanted to see him after work last night. But instead we stand together, wordless, as the katydids sing their song and the bay waves lap against the dock below.

"Travis is back from Atlanta," Malcolm says finally.

I recognize the name from one of the articles I read about the accident. He's the bassist for his old band, Gatsby.

"I heard the news from someone else. He never even called me," he says.

Could that be what's bothering him?

I squeeze his hand and he keeps talking, answering questions I've had for a while but never asked him.

"Travis was riding shotgun that day. During the tour, we rotated our seats in the van so everyone had a chance to sleep in the back rows. After that last gig, everyone was exhausted but I was pumped up on adrenaline, you know? I offered to take Jack's shift and drive. He thought he got lucky." Malcolm laughs bitterly. "Lucky. Travis and I were the only ones wearing seat belts."

I don't know what to say about the cruel randomness that took the lives of his bandmates. The ever-present guilt over how I caused my own best friend's death stirs and threatens to taunt me. In Lynn's case, the cruel randomness was her befriending me. I put my arms around Malcolm's waist and hold him tight, laying my head on his chest. He keeps talking.

"I wanted the pain to stop. Some days, I wanted everything to stop."

I think about the cuff bracelet on my wrist and what it hides. I didn't want the pain to stop. I wanted to hurt more. To punish myself for what I did.

He pulls back a little and looks down at me. "What are you doing tonight?"

I try to lighten the mood. "Tonight, as in fourteen hours from now? So far I have no plans. Why?"

"I thought maybe you could stay over again. We'll watch *Pulp Fiction* from the beginning. Maybe go for a night swim."

I know Auntsie's probably already fuming, and yet I hear myself say, "Sure. But I have to leave early to go to the shelter with my aunt."

Malcolm smiles. "We'll watch the sunrise again."

"Perfect," I say, even though I know it's not completely true.

TWENTY-ONE

When I get home, the back door is open and I smell fresh coffee, but Auntsie's bedroom door is closed. I walk through the kitchen and make enough noise on the steps to let her know I'm here, then wait a few seconds on the upstairs landing to see if her bedroom door opens. It doesn't, so I step into my room and throw my stuff on the bed. I have a little over an hour before I have to be at the Ben Franklin.

I know Auntsie wants to talk, so I leave my door open and lay back on my bed expecting to hear her footfalls on the stairs. As the moments tick by, I grow more anxious. Maybe I should go downstairs and knock on her door? Nah. She knows I'm here. She's making me sweat.

I sit up and grab my phone to search for information

about opioid addiction and recovery. I skim an article called "Supporting Those Recovering from Addiction" and see a sentence that stops my heart. Recovering addicts should avoid all alcohol. Mixing any amount of booze with an opioid could result in an overdose. It gets worse. The article says that even a small amount of an opioid could prove fatal to someone who has recently recovered and no longer has a tolerance for the drug. How recent is recent? There's so much I don't know. I reach into my pocket and clutch the bag with the pills.

What if I hadn't run into drunk Malcolm on the boardwalk that night? Or been in the garage when Tamara stopped by?

The article advises asking a doctor to prescribe Narcan. It can save the life of someone who has overdosed, but can't be self-administered. Does Malcolm carry Narcan? What good is it if he lives alone? I'm even more scared for him going on a solo tour now. Where are his parents? What do they think about all this?

I lie back down and close my eyes.

"Rough night?" I don't hear Auntsie come in.

I lay my phone facedown and nod. "Malcolm's going through some stuff."

"So are you."

"It's different for me. His old bassist is back in town. It's dredging up bad memories and guilt."

Auntsie sits on the foot of my bed. "Quinn, baby. Malcolm's problems aren't yours to solve."

"I care about him. What am I supposed to do, walk away?"

"I'm not telling you to walk away. I'm telling you to open your eyes and keep them open."

She's right. I know she's right. I nod my head slowly.

"I'm sorry I forgot to text you last night."

She pats my leg. "I remember what it was like to be so caught up in something or someone that no one else mattered."

"Auntsie, you matter."

"I matter like an aunt, not like a mom or a boyfriend."

"Auntsie…"

She shakes her head. "This isn't about me, it's about you. I'm trusting you to do the right thing. But know that if I see you making bad choices, I'm not going to stand by like some schmo and let it happen. I'm going to step in."

This is probably not the right time to tell Auntsie about Malcolm's past or that I'm staying at his house again tonight.

"Okay," I say instead. "I get it."

In the shower, I try not to think about accidental overdoses, the illusion of sunrise, or the way I feel when I lay my head against Malcolm's chest and fall asleep. Instead, I think about Auntsie. She's funny, and smart, and pretty, and much hipper than most women her age. Why isn't she someone's most important person? I wonder not only for Auntsie, but for myself. After years of being compared to her, it makes me believe that her destiny might be my own.

TWENTY-TWO

"So what's the story between you and Caleb?" I ask Auntsie as I brush through some tangles in Reggie's fur.

Auntsie bathes a Chow mix recently brought in by elderly owners who were going to assisted living and couldn't keep him. Poor Mr. Chow. I can't stand the sadness in his deep-set, black eyes.

"He's an old friend. End of story."

Auntsie's pissed at me for staying over at Malcolm's again last night. I don't blame her. I didn't exactly ask permission. I took the coward's way out and waited until she was at work to text that I wouldn't be coming home. Hope you know what you're doing was her unnerving reply. I would have preferred if she called and screamed at me. Thank goodness for satellite radio and "'90s on 9" during the car ride to Shore Paws Shelter this morning. The only other sounds were Auntsie and I breathing. She breathes very loudly when she's angry.

I keep trying.

"Old friend from high school, from college? Where did you guys meet?"

"What's with all the questions?" Auntsie turns around and places her sudsy hands on her hips. Freed from Auntsie's grip, Mr. Chow decides to give himself a nice, vigorous shake. Suds and water spray Auntsie's back and the floor. I wince. She glares.

"I'll take Reggie for a walk," I say.

Auntsie turns back to the tub. "Make it a long one." She tosses the words over her shoulder like a bucketful of hot water. Ouch.

On my way out of the shelter I run into Ben, one of the shelter managers. He's an older guy, like fifty, with a graying goatee, hip glasses, and a tribal band tat around his left bicep. This morning, I take special note of his left hand. No ring.

"Hey, Ben!" I say.

"Hey, Quinn. Where's your compadre?"

"Giving a bath to an unruly Chow mix. She could use some help. I would have given her a hand, but Reggie here really has to go."

"Then don't let me hold you up," he laughs. "I'll check on Annie and the Chow."

"Thanks!"

Reggie walks along the sidewalk with such a happy swagger—his little Chihuahua butt swaying, his pink tongue hanging from his nearly toothless mouth. I hate that he'll be going back to his cage. I take Auntsie's advice, snarky as it was, and make his walk an extra long one, giving him all the time he needs to smell all the smells and mark his territory. And maybe giving Auntsie and Ben some time to bond over the Chow.

I take a deep breath and enjoy the summer morning with my partially blind, awesomely ugly canine companion. The sky is a hazeless robin's egg blue and the air is warm but dry. A perfect beach day for people like Evie. I should take advantage of living a few blocks from the ocean before summer's over. By the time Reggie and I return to the shelter, my mind's made up. I don't care if she's not talking to me—Auntsie and I are going to the beach.

"I can't believe you got me out here before five," Auntsie says. "I'm melting."

We're sitting side by side under a red Panama Jack umbrella. I'm reading *Beloved* by Toni Morrison, and Auntsie is complaining about the sun. Our lunch at the Ocean Bay Diner was almost as silent as our car ride, so I was surprised when Auntsie agreed to come to the beach with me.

"Maybe you should take off some of those layers?" I offer.

Auntsie's wearing a Mets cap and a long sleeve rash guard, the kind the kids wear for boogie boarding.

"And fade my ink? Are you crazy?"

I put down my book. "Want to walk to the water with me? Cool off?"

She crosses her arms over her chest. "I'm good."

I trudge across the hot sand, weaving my way between camps of day-trippers and vacationers with elaborate setups, including coolers on wheels, beach tents, and baby pools. The ocean *kabooms* against the surf, muffling the laughter of swimmers as they dive under foamy whitecaps and emerge with just enough time to dive under the next one. I stand at the edge of all the excitement, letting the water pool around my feet as I sink into the wet sand.

I look back toward our umbrella to see Auntsie making her way down the sloping sand toward me. When she arrives at my side, she stares out at the water without looking my way, but I can tell she's got something on her mind.

"Ben is gay, you know." Auntsie says finally.

I shrug. "Just thought you could use some help with the Chow. I didn't think you were going to marry him." I'm practically yelling to be heard over the ocean's roar.

"Don't feel like you need to set me up with someone now that you're with Malcolm."

I open my mouth to protest, but Auntsie cuts me off.

"You're *with* Malcolm. And it's not lost on me that your mother forbade it."

"She doesn't even know him."

"No, but thanks to me, she knows the type."

I wait for more.

"Me and Caleb. I sort of lost my head over him. He was a local guy in an up-and-coming band that was generating a lot of buzz and attention from record labels. I was the same nerd girl back then that I am now, maybe nerdier. But I interviewed him for my zine and we clicked, you know? We were together for a year."

"What happened?"

"His band blew up. He got signed to a major label, recorded an album, and went on the road to promote it."

"What about you?"

"I stayed here and dealt with an unplanned pregnancy."

The world goes still. The cacophony surrounding us fades to a whirr as I try to process what Auntsie said.

"Did you? I mean, I understand if you—"

Auntsie shakes her head. "I miscarried. I know it sounds crazy, but I was sure the baby heard my thoughts. Knew I wasn't ready to be a mother. That I couldn't handle it." She stares at the horizon and keeps talking. "I broke up with Caleb during one of his calls home. He never knew why, still doesn't. At any rate, he didn't try very hard to stop me."

I have no idea what to say, but it doesn't matter because Auntsie keeps talking.

"This isn't meant to be a cautionary tale about falling in love with rockers and using backup birth control. I want you to know that I'm okay with the life I have. It's the life I earned. I don't need to be fixed up with the gay shelter manager or reunited with Caleb."

I put my arm around Auntsie and lay my head against her shoulder. She pats my hand. We stay like that for a while, watching the ocean and all the people excited by its power to lift them up and knock them down. Seems like Malcolm and I aren't the only ones who know what it's like to live with the guilt of not being careful enough with the precious lives entrusted to us.

"You know your mother had to convince me to let you stay with me?"

I'm shocked. I always thought Mom was the obstacle and Auntsie was completely on board.

"But when I suggested it, Mom got all defensive and said she needed time to think about it," I say.

"That's because she knew I'd need time to consider it. I've never cared for another living thing on my own before. I wasn't sure I could handle it. Hell, I've been volunteering at that shelter for three years and still haven't brought home a dog. Not even for a weekend."

I had wondered about that. What she told me explains a lot.

"Any one of those pooches would be lucky to have you. *I'm* lucky to have you. You deserve to be happy, Auntsie."

"So do you, Quinn baby. Even if you believe you don't." It's like Auntsie knows my thoughts and fears. "If Malcolm makes you happy, if you love him, embrace it. Enjoy every minute. But see your time together for what it is. Malcolm's already told you he has no intention of staying put. You have to learn to be happy without him too. Because you might not be able to predict which night together will be your last."

Auntsie's words bring on a slow realization.

"When you called Caleb and you asked him to give me a job..."

"It was the first time I spoke to him in twenty years."

It dawns on me what making that call cost Auntsie, and yet she was willing to dredge up her past for me. I take her hand and give it two quick squeezes. She knows I'm saying "thank you," like I know when she squeezes back it means "Anything for you, Quinn baby."

TWENTY-THREE

That night at practice, everything gels, restoring equilibrium to my world after Auntsie threw it way off-kilter.

Music rights my wrongs. It's what I loved most about being in marching band, and now this band. Eventually all the jumbled pieces come together. Whether it's a hundred band kids marching around in polyester uniforms or three misfits in a garage, there's a moment when the music clicks, when all those quarter notes and half notes add up to a whole song. It's in those moments that I feel most alive and forget how fucked up life can really be. How fucked up I can be.

"Hey, how was the wedding?" I ask Liam as we're wrapping up.

He snaps his guitar case closed.

"A lot like prom, only worse because you have to watch *old* drunk people dancing."

Malcolm laughs. I shrug.

"I never went to prom," I say.

"Too cool for prom?" Liam asks.

"No one asked." They look at me with either shock or pity—it's hard to tell. This prompts me to keep talking.

"I asked a junior, Giovanni Rivoli. Gio. He played the bass drum in marching band. I didn't like him or anything, I just figured… Anyway, he tells me, drummer to drummer, proms weren't 'his jam,' then turns around and goes with Elody Myers, another senior girl from band who played the flute."

Elaborating doesn't help with my loser image, but it's too late now. My lameness is out there.

"*Pff*. What kind of asshat would pick a flautist over a drummer?" Liam asks.

"A blind one," Malcolm says. "His loss."

"Totally," Liam agrees.

Having them jump to my defense brings sneaky tears to my eyes. I look down to blink them away.

"Hey, so we have about ten days before we're in the studio," Malcolm says, switching gears and saving me from myself. "We need to cram in as much practice as possible."

"Just tell me when. I can be here any night I'm not at Keegan's. I can also practice in the afternoon," Liam says.

We take out our phones and come up with a schedule that has us jamming almost every day or night leading up to our recording session.

Malcolm looks at me. "Quinn, you still need to write the drum part for 'That Last Night.'"

"Yeah, about that. I was thinking maybe you could write and play on that one?"

Malcolm shakes his head. "I want you to write a part that you'll be comfortable with playing live. We still have the gig, remember?"

How can I tell these guys I can't listen to that song, let alone write a drum part for it? And playing it live? Forget it. But I don't want to get into it right now. One tale of woe from Quinn is enough for one night.

"Okay, I'll come up with something."

"Good," Malcolm says.

"I'm going to take off," Liam says. "Keeks is waiting. She's not going to be happy about this rehearsal schedule."

"Invite her to the recording session," Malcolm says. "Maybe it'll help if she feels part of it."

"Yeah?" Liam asks.

"Of course." Malcolm turns to me. "Invite your aunt too. We'll have her sit in on cowbell."

"She'll love you forever," I say.

"That's the plan," Malcolm says.

I linger for a while after Liam leaves. Malcolm wants me to stay the night, but I tell him I can't.

"Auntsie and I got into a thing earlier today. I should go home."

He takes my face in his hands and kisses me on the lips, gently at first and then with more urgency. I'm tingling.

"You sure?"

"No, I'm not sure. But it's the right thing to do."

"Come on then. I'll walk you to your car."

I'm relieved he doesn't press me because my resolve is breaking. The two times I slept here, sure, we fooled around, but mostly we slept. We're not "sleeping together." We're sleeping. Together. And I'm already used to it—waking up next to him. Auntsie's words about not knowing what night would be our last aren't lost on me as we walk hand in hand to my car. Malcolm opens the door for me. I hope I'm not making a mistake by leaving.

I roll down my window after buckling myself in. Malcolm leans in and kisses me one more time. Then he stares at me for a few seconds.

"Quinn?"

"Yeah?"

"I would have asked you to prom."

I smile at him even though we both have no way of knowing if that would have happened.

"I would have said yes."

I watch him in the rearview mirror as I pull away. He's standing in the street with one hand in his pocket, the other raised in goodbye. It takes everything I have not to put the car in reverse.

TWENTY-FOUR

As it turns out, that Sunday night, when Malcolm said he would have asked me to prom, was the last time we slept apart. I've been sleeping over at Malcolm's ever since, and it's all still very PG-13. What we have is better than sex. I like watching movies and kissing on the couch until we fall asleep. I love the rhythm of him breathing beside me—the way he protectively drapes his arm across my belly at night and kisses my cheek before slipping out of bed to watch the sun rise.

It's the perfect arrangement for someone like me, who's gone too far too fast and gotten burned, and an insomniac like Malcolm. He says he hasn't slept this well since before the accident.

The only one who's not happy is Auntsie.

"I was talking to your bed the other day. It misses you."

That's what she said yesterday when I stopped home to have dinner with her between work at the Ben Franklin and band practice. Point taken.

"I'll be home more once we're done recording," I told her.

So far, Malcolm's been awesome about respecting my unspoken boundaries. But on Friday night, while we were kissing in the shallow end of his heated, in-ground pool, he indirectly brings up the subject of wanting more. I'm not surprised. The sensation of his lips on my neck, his skin against mine, it's almost got me second-guessing my reborn chastity.

"I think we may need to renegotiate the terms of our original deal," Malcolm whispers in my ear. The brush of his beard against my neck gives me shivers.

"You mean the part about you sleeping naked in my bed?" I tease.

He kisses me softly on the lips. "I mean the part about you sleeping naked in mine."

"You sleep on a couch."

"True. But I still think we need an addendum."

I smile and pull away from him, falling backward underwater. Malcolm dives under me and in one sleek motion scoops me into his arms before I can float away. He stands up, and I wrap my arms around his neck. Then he kisses me while sinking down lower in the water, so that our shoulders are submerged. The steamy water warms my goose bumps.

"If you're not ready to reopen talks, just say so," he says.

I let one arm fall from his neck and weave it back and forth underwater as I look around. This borrowed house, this borrowed time, it's enough for now. Sex would only complicate things, make it harder to give back what isn't mine.

"We can't renegotiate. Not when our original contract is still in attorney review."

"It is? How long does attorney review last?"

Until I'm sure we're each other's most important person.

"It may take a while."

"It's okay, Cat's Eye. I can wait." He kisses me one more time, then lets my legs gently fall into the water. "Come on, let's go watch a movie. You pick tonight."

"I want to shower off first."

Malcolm raises his eyebrows.

"Alone." I clarify.

"I'll make the popcorn."

The next morning, I open my eyes to find Malcolm propped on one elbow staring at me.

"What?" Instinctively I reach for my hair and smooth down my bed head. I knew I should have blown it dry before the movie.

"Why are you afraid to write the drum part for 'That Last Night?'"

We've only got five full days before we start recording, and I know Malcolm and Liam are anxious to rehearse it.

I sit up, defensive, and Malcolm adjusts himself so he's sitting beside me.

"I'm not afraid. In fact, I had an idea for a different arrangement that would require minimal drums…"

Malcolm takes both of my hands in his and flips my palms upward. My eyes instinctively move to my cuff bracelet and Malcolm's follow. He runs his thumb along the leather bracelet, inching toward the snap that holds my secret. I pull my hands away, and Malcolm raises his in surrender.

"I'm sorry, I shouldn't have… Can you talk about it? Can you tell me what happened to your friend?"

Panic rises in my chest. My scalp gets the familiar pins-and-needles feeling, and I have to close my eyes to slow my breathing. I rock back and forth a little and squeeze my wrist with my bracelet between my legs. When Malcolm's arms encircle me, I lean back against him.

"I've got you."

He does. His touch makes my anxiety subside. No need to fumble for my Xanax. I'm safe. Safe enough to start talking.

"There's this hill in my town—we called it Mount Doom. Corny, I know. Most kids can only bike about halfway up before petering out and walking their bikes the rest of the way to the top."

I draw a diagram in the air with my finger—one that looks

like a two-humped camel or a woman's cleavage—as I explain how getting up Mount Doom means peddling really fast down one hill, crossing a really busy intersection, and peddling up the other side.

"You have to time the intersection just right. You don't want to stop and lose speed, but you have to watch for oncoming cars too. I got really good at it." I take a deep breath, still hesitant, giving myself over to the memory. "Lynn and I were freshmen. It was the first warm day, when everyone heads outside after school with baseball mitts and skateboards. Lynn wanted to go to the library. She had a book on hold that she wanted to pick up. But I talked her into riding bikes. And so, of course, that meant tackling Mount Doom. I was so immature. And stupid."

I tell Malcolm how Lynn was right beside me as we crested the first hill. How I thought she stayed beside me as I sped downward, gaining speed, the chilly March air stinging my face.

"There was a point where I had to take my feet off the pedals because they were turning too fast. I looked both ways at the intersection, making sure there were no cars. I yelled to Lynn. Urged her on. I zoomed across the street and charged up the other side. When I glanced back, Lynn had fallen farther behind than I thought…"

I trail off, so lost in remembering that I'm unaware that I'm still talking.

In that brief moment that I looked over my shoulder, I saw the SUV coming closer, saw Lynn racing down the hill. Saw them both like dots on a grid, about to collide. I opened my mouth to scream. I did scream, "no" or "stop!" or "wait!" or all three of them. It didn't change what happened. No one heard me. Why didn't anyone hear me? Maybe I never screamed at all.

Pieces of bike flew everywhere... Lynn's helmet, Lynn's black Converse. Lynn. Poor broken Lynn. Why did she listen to me? I got off my bike. My fingers fumbled to dial 911. Our moms arrived while I was sitting on the curb, clutching one of Lynn's sneakers, tears and snot streaming down my face. The guttural screams. The look on Lynn's mother's face...

I shake my head.

"I caused it. All of it. The sadness, the grief. I ruined her mother's life. I ruined my mother's life. There's no way to say 'I'm sorry' for something like that. No way to make it right."

I take off my bracelet and expose the scar it hides. The whitish, pinkish skin is raised and rough and looks like a Christian cross lying on its side. Malcolm doesn't say anything. He doesn't have to. He knew all along. He has tears in his eyes when he takes my wrist and brings it to his lips, gently kissing the spot where life almost ran out of me.

My chest heaves and I begin to sob uncontrollably. Malcolm holds me, lets me know he won't let me fall apart.

"Shhhhh, I got you," he whispers. I'm thankful he doesn't lie and say everything's going to be all right. He doesn't tell me to stop crying either, just lets it happen until I've exhausted myself.

"What would you say to her if you could see her again?" Malcolm asks when I'm finally calm.

I wipe my eyes and think about it. There's so much. Too much. I want to tell her I'm sorry. So, so, sorry. That I wish it was me instead of her. I want to tell her I miss her, to fill her in on all that's happened since she's been gone, to give her back the life she missed out on. I want to tell her I love her.

"I…" I start to tell Malcolm all of this, but he puts a finger to my lips.

"Don't tell me. Say it with 'That Last Night.' It's yours now. Do whatever you want with it. Change the lyrics, change the guitar part, whatever it takes to say what you need to say."

I spend my entire shift at the Ben Franklin running the song in my head and thinking about Lynn. I almost break down when I sell a cheap friendship bracelet to some tween girl holding a quilted sunflower change purse that Lynn would've loved. On my break, I walk down to the gazebo by the bay where Malcolm and I shared breakfast a few weeks ago. With my earbuds in, I listen to the song that was Malcolm's attempt to deal with a profound loss and has now become mine. It should begin with a piano or maybe an organ, and vocals. Keys and Malcolm, that's all it needs for the first two verses. After that, I hear strings, maybe an upright bass and cello. No drums or guitar. Not yet.

I wasn't making excuses when I told Malcolm there should be minimal drums. The song will be half over before Liam chimes in with electric guitar and I start to play, only hi-hat at first, then toms. I've changed my mind about a gospel choir. It's impractical and would probably be overbearing. But it needs backing vocals. Female backing vocals or maybe a few choirboys.

At practice that night, I run through my ideas with Liam and Malcolm, singing my way through the parts. My hands shake a little and I'm self-conscious about my pitchy voice, nervous about exposing so much of myself to Liam and Malcolm, but their faces exude warmth and understanding, and somehow I get through. When I'm done, I find it hard to look at them, but Liam breaks the silence and puts me at ease.

"So…for the female backing vocals. Who were you thinking?" Liam asks.

I laugh because Liam is trying so hard to be delicate and tactful, and neither is in his DNA.

"Don't worry, not me. I was thinking my sister and her friends from choir."

Liam clutches his chest in mock relief. "Oh, thank God, because there's no amount of auto-tuning that could fix that."

I kind of love him right now, but instead of telling him that, I throw a drumstick at his head. He ducks and it misses. I need to keep up my front.

"Q, watch it. I almost lost an eye!"

I turn to Malcolm, who hasn't said anything yet. "So what do you think?"

Malcolm stays silent. He's stroking his beard and has this faraway look on his face.

"Malcolm? If you hate my ideas, I totally understand—"

He snaps out of it. "No, no. I like your ideas. Really like them, actually. It's just the recording session is so tight. The only way we'd be able to record all the instruments and vocals is live."

"I know not of what you speak. Don't we record everything live?" I ask.

Liam jumps in to explain. "We track the parts, Q. One instrument at a time. We'll record drums first. Vocals are usually last."

"That's right," Malcolm says. "You'll play drums to my rough demo and then Liam and I will use your drum part to record our parts. But with keys, guitar, cello, backing vocals, and did you say upright bass?"

I nod.

"We'll have to play all together, live, in the studio. We'll need time to rehearse there and then after that, we'll have to get it right with only one or two takes." Malcolm's pacing. "I'll play keys, maybe a Moog organ sound, and the vocals. You think your sister and her friends can do it?"

"I'll ask. I can see about a cellist too. I know a girl who played in my high school's orchestra," I say. "Do you play upright bass?"

Malcolm shakes his head. "Even if I did, we need another

body to record. I know who I can ask. I'm not sure what he'll say though." He runs his fingers through his hair as he circles the garage. "There's a lot of moving parts here. I'm still not sure—"

"I love the idea of recording live." Liam beams, and his grin infects Malcolm. "We can do this."

Malcolm stops mid-pace. "You know what? You're right. Fuck it. Let's do it. What's the worst that can happen?"

I've learned never to tempt the universe with that question, but I'm not going to let my silly superstitions squash his excitement.

Liam leans over and fist-bumps me. "Nice work, Q. This is going to be awesome. As long as you don't sing."

TWENTY-FIVE

I can listen to Ricky Keyes talk all day. That's what I'm thinking shortly after arriving at Atlantic Trax, this totally high-end recording studio in Asbury Park. The mixture of Nashville and cigarettes in Ricky's voice is hypnotically charming. He could very well be The Quinn Whisperer.

"Lay your vision on me, man," Ricky says.

We're meeting with Ricky in a room that looks like NASA's ground control meets the cockpit of the Starship *Enterprise*. The soundboard, with hundreds of dials and levers, is easily the length and width of a grand piano and is flanked on either side by two flat screen monitors. Behind the board, a step up, are two high-back leather seats, which give the producer—or Captain Kirk—a better vantage point through the glass window into the main recording studio.

Ricky nods enthusiastically, making notes on a yellow legal pad and interjecting phrases like "far out" and "right on" as Malcolm lays out our three-day recording plan. It's like Ricky borrows all the cool from generations past, but it totally works for him.

"It's going to be tight, dude, but we can do this," Ricky says.

It's around noon on Friday, "morning" in rocker-speak. We're about to start recording Malcolm's five-song demo. I'm amped up, nervous, and, okay, slightly crushing on Ricky. I see why Auntsie got so excited when Malcolm mentioned him.

Ricky looks down at his legal pad, on which he's drawn three stacked boxes, and made some notes.

"So day one will be drums, scratch vocals, and bass. Day two, mostly guitar and vocals. We'll also use day two to punch up any bass parts that need fixing." He doodles in the margins as he thinks. "Let's see... Sometime in the early morning hours of day three we'll record your live track. And I'll need the rest of Sunday for mixing." He looks up at us and smiles. "Y'all didn't plan on sleeping, did ya?"

Liam and I laugh a little, but Malcolm is serious.

"He's not kidding."

"Sound like a plan?" Ricky asks.

"Sounds like a plan," Malcolm says.

"Right on." Ricky looks back and forth between Liam and Malcolm. "Who's laying down the drum track?"

I raise my hand tentatively, like I'm in school. "Uh, that would be me."

"You got a name, Me?" he jokes.

"Quinn Gallo." I put out my hand.

He takes my hand in both of his. "Quinn Gallo. Very rock and roll. The drums are all mic'd and ready to go. Good move using the studio's kit. It's gonna save us a shit load of time."

Ricky explains how a different mic gets attached to each drum, with additional microphones hung overhead in the booth to capture the sound of the whole kit.

"The drum tracks will serve as the foundation. The first layer to the entire recording session," Ricky says.

"You're like the noodle foundation for a lasagna made of sound," Liam explains to me like I'm three.

"I guess that would make you the cheese," I joke.

Ricky bursts out laughing. "I love Jersey girls."

Ten minutes later, I'm ensconced behind the studio's drum kit in a room by myself with a rectangular window that looks out onto an additional recording space for the vocalist and rest of the band. Beyond *that* room is the control room, where Ricky, Liam, and Malcolm are standing behind the soundproof glass. They seem very far away with a whole room between us. I've got on headphones so I can hear Malcolm's songs—the same recordings I've been practicing to since the beginning of August. That's what I'll be playing along to.

I adjust my glasses, crack my neck and knuckles, and shake out my arms like an Olympic swimmer about to dive into a pool. Ricky switches on the mic in the booth and I hear him in my headphones.

"Ready?"

I give him a thumbs-up.

Malcolm leans into the mic, and I hear him in my head before Ricky cues up the music.

"You got this."

Do I? I feel so isolated and lonely, yet at the same time, on display, like a penguin at the aquarium. My nerves get the best of me on the first track, and we do at least five takes of that one before I get it close to right. I can't seem to get in the pocket. Oddly, it's advice from Liam that finally gets my head in the game.

"Don't look at us," Liam says through the mic. "Close your eyes and pretend you're in the garage."

Normally, I hate it when Liam's right, but in this case I'm too relieved to care. His advice works, and I get through the rest of the tracks pretty smoothly. But it still takes *forever* and there are a few bumps here and there. Ricky tells me not to worry about minor changes in tempo and volume. He can go back and fix them later.

After we get the drum parts down, I hang in the control room with Ricky while Malcolm and Liam go into the main recording room. Ricky is as easy to talk to as he is to listen to.

"I'm focusing mainly on getting Malcolm's bass parts right now, but we'll record Liam and some scratch vocals at the same time. Every once in a while you get lucky, and the guitarist will be okay with the scratch recording, but most of the time? Guitarists and vocalists are—"

"Perfectionists?" I offer.

"I was going to say OCD divas, but yeah, *perfectionists*. Your way is nicer."

Sitting behind the soundboard with Ricky is fascinating. It's five times the size of what we use at Keegan's. The weird part is, even though there are all these levers and knobs to make adjustments to the sound, Ricky watches the pulsing levels on the screens and uses a laptop to make all the changes.

"Sometimes I do sound at the club where I work," I tell Ricky.

"A drummer and a sound gal. Way to play against type, Quinn Gallo."

I never thought about it that way. "I guess there aren't many female sound engineers?"

"Nope. Women in the music production business are like unicorns. In all my years doing this, I've met exactly two."

"Women or unicorns?"

Ricky laughs. "You're all right, Quinn Gallo."

I stay pretty quiet for the rest of the recording session, taking in what I can and asking an occasional question. Weirdly, the whole recording process has me spending more time with Ricky than anyone else. Malcolm and I are quite literally isolated from each other most of the time and more than that, he seems distant. Or maybe *focused* is a better word. Whatever it is, no one would ever guess we've been spending every night together by the way he's been interacting with me here. I get it. I think. Here I'm Quinn the Drummer, not Quinn the whatever it is I am to Malcolm. This is more than a recording project for him—it's his future. His second chance to get back what he lost. Still, I wouldn't mind a hand squeeze or a hug every now and then.

Shortly before we break for food, I feel compelled to warn Ricky that Auntsie will be arriving soon with baked ziti.

"She's kind of a rabid fan. She interviewed you once, for her zine, a long time ago."

"Well, all right! What's not to love about a rabid fan? Especially one who comes bearing Italian food."

Auntsie arrives about ten minutes after Kiki. She's surprisingly restrained when I reintroduce her to Ricky about an hour later in the kitchen/break room. She is, however, wearing more makeup then usual and a black, sleeveless dress that accentuates her ink. They shake hands, she tells him she's a longtime fan of his work as a songwriter and producer, then wastes no time doling out heaping portions of baked ziti and garlic bread to everyone gathered around the table.

"Eat it while it's still warm," she says. She made two huge trays, enough for seconds and then some. (The Gallo women aren't happy unless everyone is stuffed, and there's still tons of leftovers.) Although with the way Liam is scarfing down Auntsie's signature pasta dish, there may be none left.

"Aunt of Q, this sauce may be better than my dad's," Liam says through a mouthful. Then he points his fork in her direction. "Please don't tell him I said that."

Auntsie pretends to lock her lips and throw away the key, then plops another spoonful on Liam's plate.

"Here, have some more." Then she turns to Kiki with a full serving spoon. "You too, hon. Love the hair, by the way."

Kiki reaches for her blue bangs.

"Thanks, did it myself." Kiki wants to be a hairstylist and is already taking classes at beauty school. She wants to do some kind of balayage to my long, dark hair. I keep telling her I'll think about it even though I have no idea what the heck she's talking about or what that is.

Satisfied that everyone's full, Auntsie stands to leave. "So I'll be back with your sister and her friends tomorrow. Any idea of the timing?" Evie's driving down from North Jersey in the morning with her two choir friends.

Ricky answers. "Probably not before ten at night. We need time to rehearse before we record. Be prepared to pull an all-nighter."

Auntsie looks shocked, but tries to play it cool as she walks out the door. "I'll tell them to pack their toothbrushes. Ciao!"

After we eat, Malcolm and Liam return to the recording

booth and I hang with Keeks for a bit. She decided to stay until Liam is finished.

"Let's go for coffee," she says. "I know a place on the boardwalk."

Outside, daylight is fading but there's plenty of time before sunset.

"I expected it to be dark already," I tell Kiki as we walk along sipping our lattes. I lost all track of time in the windowless studio.

I watch some beachgoers packing it in for the day while others arrive with volleyballs and beach chairs to enjoy the twilight hours by the ocean. Music drifts from one of the patio bars, an interesting mix of drums and pan flute. I breathe in the familiar boardwalk smells—onions, peppers, suntan lotion, the ocean—and I'm struck once again with the feeling that I'm missing out.

"Soooo," Keeks says. "You and Malcolm."

I smile in spite of myself. Because even though I never expected it, I like the sound of it.

"Yeah, me and Malcolm."

"Are things getting serious? Are you officially boyfriend and girlfriend?"

Is this what it feels like to be someone's girlfriend? I'm an expert in unrequited love, but for whatever Malcolm and I are, I have no reference point.

"I'm not sure. We spend a lot of time together, but it's still kind of new and, well, after Labor Day, he's leaving and my own existence post-summer is still up in the air."

I explain that I'd like to move in permanently with my aunt, but I'm not sure it will happen.

"Well, selfishly, I hope you stay. Liam and all our friends are leaving for college soon and I'll be stuck in Seaside, alone. It will be nice to know you're only one town over. The off-season is going to be lonelier than usual."

"Rutgers isn't that far. You'll see Liam on weekends, right?"

Kiki nods slowly. "Yes, but it won't be the same. We've lived in the same tiny town our whole lives. Known each other since pre-K. Don't tell him, but I think I've loved him since then too." Kiki laughs, and I'm touched by her honesty. "Soon Liam will be meeting all these new people and having all these *college* experiences. What if he decides I don't fit in with his new life?"

I guess it's possible college will break up Keeks and Liam. What if it's like Malcolm said, and some people are only meant to be together for a certain amount of time? What if that time together is also contingent upon being in the same place? I don't share this with Kiki, mostly because I don't want to believe it. I'm feeling very protective of her all of a sudden.

"Liam adores you, Keeks. And who else is going to put up with his Liam-ness the way you do?"

Kiki clinks her plastic cup with mine. "You're a good

person, Quinny. No wonder Liam was so anxious to set you up with Andrew. I'm still worried though. I trust Liam, but girls have been known to throw themselves at him. I should know. I was one of them."

While I understand her fears and share her nervousness about being apart from someone you care about, with Malcolm, it's not the girls I worry about. It's the drugs. Yes, it would suck if I lost Malcolm to someone else, but that would be inconsequential next to losing him to an accidental overdose. I do not want another friend to die on my watch.

"I'm thinking I might want to go with Malcolm in the fall."

"Quinny, that's awesome! You two *are* getting serious. Why didn't you say so before?"

Uh, because I just decided right now?

"Please don't tell anyone. You're the only one who knows. My aunt and sister won't be happy, my mother will be apoplectic, and Malcolm… I'm not sure he even wants me to go."

"You'll never know unless you talk to him about it," Kiki says.

We pass by a small blue building, adorned with a mural with mystical images—a giant eye, a crystal ball.

"Or we could get our palms read? Find out what's in the cards for you and Malcolm? Liam's sister, Lucy, went there last year, and this psychic, Madame Ava, practically told her she'd end up with her current boyfriend, Connor. Lucy dated Andrew, you know. And as much as I wanted them to stay together, you could tell there was something missing. They were more like best friends than anything more. Anyway, we should do it."

I stop for a second and peer inside the building. The waiting area is full. I check the time, half consider going in, but decide against it.

"Maybe next time. Looks like there's a long wait," I say.

Really, I'm not sure I'm ready to hear what Madame Ava has to say.

TWENTY-SIX

Later that night, or more like during the wee hours of Saturday morning, I'm lying on the couch wrapped in Malcolm. My insecurities about his aloofness while we were at the studio are fading. We're half dozing, half watching a movie, and I'm relieved to have him so close and all to myself after spending twelve strange hours in the studio.

Tomorrow will be more of the same. Liam will be recording his guitar parts, Malcolm will do his final vocals, and I'll try to hold my shit together as I chill with Ricky and wait for my sister and her two friends from chorus to arrive with Auntsie. The cellist, Olivia, is driving herself here.

"I'm scared," I say softly.

"Of?" Malcolm whispers back.

Everything?

"Recording tomorrow."

"Don't be. You're holding your own so far, and the arrangement you worked out for 'That Last Night' is awesome. We've got time to do a couple of takes and after that, Ricky can fix whatever's not perfect."

"Wouldn't it be great if we all had producers in real life? Someone to smooth out our rough edges and imperfections, make us better?"

"The studio isn't real life."

I'm happy to hear him say that, because I don't like the dynamics between us when we're there. Here, I feel safe, secure, like the bad stuff that's already happened and any future disasters that await can't touch us. In the studio, I was constantly on edge, teetering between greatness and complete disaster. In the final analysis, I'd gladly give up greatness for the predictability of this couch.

Malcolm continues talking about producers. "Anyway, I like rough edges and imperfections. It's what makes a person interesting. It's what makes a guy walk into a bar on a random night, see a girl with a book and ugly glasses and think, *Now there's a girl I could fall I love with.*"

My body freezes. It's like Malcolm dropped a verbal orangutan into the quarter inch space between us. I sense him (Malcolm, not the orangutan) waiting for response. I turn over and lay one hand on his cheek, then give his whiskers a little tug.

"You think my glasses are ugly?"

He nods. "But your eyes are beautiful. You're beautiful."

The way he looks at me, it's almost more than I can take. I feel naked, exposed, unworthy of his undivided attention. I bite my lip to keep from looking away and lay my forehead against his.

"I want to go with you," I blurt out.

He's confused at first, then smiles. "You're serious?" Is he shocked or hopeful by my non sequitur? Should I have said something about love?

"I'm serious. I want to go with you on tour, even if it's not as your drummer. I can be your manager, your roadie, your groupie—"

Malcolm kisses me slow and deep. I arch my back and wrap my arms around his neck.

"Save the sales pitch, Cat's Eye," he says when we separate. "You're in. You. Me. Twenty-three clubs in twelve weeks."

I'm in. I pause for a second, waiting to regret making a life-altering decision in the time it takes most people to select a latte flavor. But all I feel is relief, the kind I haven't felt since falling asleep while studying for my chemistry final and arriving at school the next day to find out it had been postponed. My "solid life plan" will have to wait, and everyone will be pissed at me, but none of that matters. This is more important. Malcolm's second chance and sobriety are at stake. I'm not going to be careless with another friend.

I kiss Malcolm again, then snuggle against him to resume watching the movie. A little while later, I fall into a peaceful, dreamless sleep—the kind I used to have when I was a kid, before my foray into fuckupery made it impossible to sleep soundly again.

TWENTY-SEVEN

The next sixteen hours in the studio feel like we've stepped out of the real world and into a Salvador Dalí painting, the one with the melting clocks on a barren landscape. The studio's fluorescent glow and arctic air-conditioning make it difficult to keep track of hours, days, and seasons. Is it still summer out there? It reminds me of being in bed with the flu—the outside world seems shrouded and far away.

There are sooo many takes of Liam's guitar parts and Malcolm's vocals. Liam corrects every miniscule mistake. Malcolm refuses to be auto-tuned. It's exhausting for me, and all I'm doing is sitting here with Kiki and Ricky, adding my two cents every now and then.

"Do you think this take sounded better than the last one?" Kiki asks.

"My ears have been so corrupted I can't even tell anymore," I say.

I'm restless, but also impressed by Malcolm's and Liam's determination to get their parts exactly right, not to mention Ricky's patience to make it happen. We move around in a sleep-deprived haze, dividing our time between food breaks, cigarette breaks (for Ricky and Malcolm), nap breaks, coffee breaks, fresh air breaks, and finally, one big break after Liam's and Malcolm's parts are officially done. It's during that break that Ricky listens to a rough recording of "That Last Night," which Malcolm created based on my arrangement. He sang all the harmonies and played every instrument—using a keyboard to create the upright bass and cello sounds. It sounds exactly like what I constructed in my head.

"Righteous," Ricky says, beaming. He's sitting behind the console in one of the commander chairs. Malcolm, Liam, Kiki, and I are sitting on a red velvet couch behind him. "This might be our single."

"I wrote the basic melody and lyrics. Quinn turned it into something better and bigger than I imagined." He squeezes my hand and I offer a half smile.

Kiki's mouth has been hanging open since the song finished. "Quinny! You never told me you could do this!"

"I better watch it," Ricky says to me. "You might put me out of a job."

Things happen fast after that. Auntsie arrives with Evie, the choir girls, and dessert sometime after ten. Olivia, the cellist, gets there soon after. Shortly before midnight, we're set up and ready to rehearse our parts, but there's still no sign of the bassist, so Ricky winds up filling in. This guy is a genius.

"Take a break," Ricky says after we've run through the song about ten times. "Get some fresh air, clear out the cobwebs, have a Coke and one of these delicious cookies. Are these snickerdoodles?"

Auntsie nods.

"Right on," says Ricky.

I don't want a snickerdoodle. What I'd really like is to spend a few minutes alone with Malcolm, to center myself before we record. I'm about to suggest we go someplace quiet when the studio door opens and in walks a lanky guy with sandy blond, tousled hair carrying a six-pack of Bud Light.

"Travis!" Malcolm says, extending his hand. "What up, bro? I didn't think you were coming. You know Ricky."

Travis? Travis who was riding shotgun with Malcolm when their bandmates were killed? Travis who blew back into town and never bothered to call Malcolm? Travis who knows Malcolm went to rehab and walks in carrying beer? *Pff.* Travis. I wish I'd known he's who Malcolm had asked to record this song. It's a reminder that whatever we may share, this project is all his.

Travis looks around as he shakes Ricky's hand. "The place hasn't changed much since the last time we were here."

Malcolm does a quick round of introductions, then pulls Travis aside. "Let me play the song for you. The bass part is easy. Feel free to improvise. We can run through it with Quinn when you're ready."

Travis gives me no more than a cursory glance before turning back to Malcolm. "Know what man? How about I run through it with just you and… What did you say your name was?" he says, looking at Liam.

Travis's cold disinterest is shifting the entire mood of this recording session, and I don't like it.

Liam shoots me a subtle look before he answers. "Liam."

"Right, Liam." Travis twists the top off one of the bottles and offers it to Liam and Ricky. When they decline, he hands it to Malcolm, then opens one for himself. I don't want one, but he doesn't offer me a drink. They clink bottles, and Malcolm takes a sip.

"It's good to have you here, man," he says while clapping Travis on the shoulder. When Malcolm takes another sip of beer, my hands reflexively ball into fists. He catches my eye, but when I give him a frown that says *WTF* he merely turns away.

In that instant, it's like a steel security door comes crashing down, leaving Kiki and I on the outside. I take a deep breath, frustrated by this male bonding ritual that's challenging Malcolm's precarious sobriety.

"Come on, Keeks. Let's take coffee orders and get out of here," I say.

The stand on the boardwalk is closed, so Kiki winds up driving us two towns over to a twenty-four-hour Dunkin' Donuts. On the way back to the studio, I'm anxious about being gone for too long. The salty air wafts through the open car windows, brushing against my skin and sending a chill down my spine—the kind that Grammy says means someone's walking over your grave. I shiver.

Keeks's eyes dart toward me as she drives. "You okay?"

"Just nervous about recording this last song."

She puts a hand on my shoulder. "Don't worry, Quinny. The rehearsal went well. You're going to be amazing."

I wish I shared Kiki's confidence as we ride the elevator up to the third floor, carrying two disposable trays with coffee for everyone except the cellist. She brought her own hot tea in a thermos. *We should have gotten the Box O' Joe*, I think. It would have been more efficient. Too late now.

When we reach our floor, Kiki and I put the coffees down in the kitchen, then I look for my bag and drumsticks, which I left in the cubbyhole storage area out in the hall. That's where I see Malcolm. I smile and am about to call out to him, but my breath catches in my throat.

He's digging through my bag!

He's so focused he doesn't know I'm here. I stay where I am. I couldn't move if I wanted to. I know what he's looking for. I see his shoulders relax. He's found it. That's when he looks up and sees me down the hall.

"Find what you're looking for?" I don't even try to hide my hurt and anger as I walk toward him.

He closes his hand around the small Ziploc bag. "Quinn, it's not... I was just looking for Advil. My hand has been killing me for the last ten hours. I forgot these were even in here."

Seriously? Is he going to stand there and lie to me? I call him out. "If you were looking for Advil, you would have waited until I came back and asked me. Instead, you sneak around like some kind of—"

The word "junkie" falls into the silence between us.

The expression on his face tells me I'm right. He knows he's caught. I move toward him and put out my hand. He hesitates for a few beats before giving me the bag.

"What are you going to do with those?" he asks. I don't like the fear in his voice or the fact the he's more focused on the pills than what he just did.

"Flush them down the toilet. I should have done that in the first place." I turn to leave, and he grabs my arm a little too roughly.

"Quinn, wait."

I shrug away and glare at him. "What?"

"Keep one, just one. Please? Being here again, recording

without those guys, it's been hard for me. My hand *is* hurting, and it's dredging up the old pain. When Travis walked in, I…I'm worried I won't be able to finish without some help."

"Help? Like the beer Travis gave you? *I'm* not giving you anything that could lead to a major setback, or worse. You know alcohol's a trigger, and you also know better than to mix it with an opioid."

"It was a few sips, and FYI, I don't need an NA lecture from you."

I cross my arms to keep from smacking him. I am seriously, seriously pissed. "And I don't need you rummaging through my stuff and grabbing my arm to get what you want."

He throws up his arms, a mixture of anger and exasperation.

Back at ya, I want to scream. Instead, I walk way.

"Quinn, wait. You're right. Okay? I'm being a jerk. But I need this one little favor. Who else am I supposed to ask?"

I'm pissed, but I still pity him. I hate that I pity him.

"It's not a little favor. What you're asking—" I lower my voice. "It's dangerous. You've been *drinking*."

"It was only a few sips," he says again. Agitated, he runs a hand through his hair.

"You've come so far. You're better than this."

"I *am* better. That's why I can handle it now. One pill, Quinn. Just one to get me over this hump. Afterward, I'll be strong enough to walk away."

I shake my head. "Nope. Sorry. Not going to do it."

His voice rises. "Why are you being like this? I asked you to hold those for me. They're mine. They're not yours to throw away."

An ugly realization hits me. "Is that why you've wanted me around? I thought you wanted to be close to me, not these." I hold up the bag. "I get it now. I was your human safety net. Keeper of the pills."

My comment smacks some reality into Malcolm.

"What? No! You're not my human safety net."

"No? Then what am I to you, Malcolm? I'd really like to know."

His face darkens, and his sudden mood shift scares me.

"I don't know what you are to me, *Quinn*. But right now you're doing a really great job of acting like my mother."

He spits out my name like poison. My *name*, not Cat's Eye. Tears well up in my eyes. I have no words.

"I told you not to do this. I told you not to save me," he whisper-yells. "I knew this would happen."

"That what would happen?"

He waves his arms back and forth between us.

"This. Me and you. Last night, when you told me you wanted to come on the road with me?" He shakes his head. "At first I was happy, but then I thought about it. This is too much. I've got the tour to think about, the showcase for my old label. This is not the time to fall in love. Maybe after the tour—"

His words knock me back to the person I was at the beginning of the summer, the one whose "relationships" had only happened in her head. *I'm going back to Austria*, Ralph said. *I have my career to think about*, Mr. G said. *Maybe after the tour*, Malcolm said.

When Malcolm said he could wait, I thought he was talking about sex, not a relationship. I cross my arms over my chest and look down, allowing the hot tears that have been blurring my vision fall from my eyes.

Ricky pops his head out of the control room. "We're ready in five," he says.

"Be right there," Malcolm calls. When he sees I'm crying, his face softens and he takes a step forward. "Quinn, I said that wrong—"

"No, you said it exactly right, Malcolm. I didn't mean to be so inconvenient." I throw the bag of pills at him. "Here. Why don't you ask your mother to hold those for you?" I push past him and grab my bag. "I need my drumsticks."

"Cat's Eye, please." He sounds like himself again, like the Malcolm from last night who hinted that he was in love with me, not the one who tried to take that love away. But it's too late. He's shown me another side of himself, one that reminds me of the other guys who made it very clear I was not their most important person. It was a joke to think I could be his.

"You know what? I can't do this," I say.

"What do you mean? We need you to record this song."

"I wasn't talking about the song."

I turn, prepared to make a dramatic exit, and smack into

Liam. I wonder how much he's heard. From the look on his face? Everything. He gives my arm a squeeze, and I lift one corner of my mouth.

"You going to be okay?" he asks softly.

I nod, too afraid to speak, then walk past him to find my sister and Auntsie. They're in the kitchen. Auntsie immediately sees I've been crying and knows something's very wrong.

"Do you want to talk about it?"

I shake my head and close my eyes. "Can you take me home after we record?" I ask. "I don't think Malcolm needs me. After the song, we're done."

She hugs me, understands me. For a split second, I consider my small white pill in my back pocket. *You're better than that*, I say to myself. *A pill isn't going to fix what you're feeling right now.* And in my case, I know it's true.

Evie rubs my back. "Whatever happened, I'm sure it's his fault. Come on, let's get in there," she says soothingly. "I can't believe I'm in a recording studio and living the rock and roll dream. Woohoo!"

Her excitement lightens my mood. I put my arm around her.

"I can't believe you're up past midnight...and that you unironically said, 'Woohoo.'"

TWENTY-EIGHT

I'm back in my isolation chamber, ready to record. Everyone else is set up in the main studio. Ricky explained that we have to record this way so the mics for the vocals and other instruments don't pick up the sound of the drum. It's fine. Perfect, actually. The only way I'm going to get through this is if I'm not in the same room as Malcolm.

From my vantage point, I can see the profiles of Liam, my sister, and her friends. Ricky, Kiki, and Auntsie are in the control room facing me. Malcolm, Travis, and the cellist are on the opposite side of the studio, out of sight. Good.

Ricky talks into the microphone. It's weird to see his lips moving behind the glass while hearing him in my headphones.

"Let's light it up!" He holds up his hand, a combination

of a maestro and the guy who starts a drag race, and counts us in. "Three, two, one…"

He swings his arm down in one sudden motion, and we begin.

Malcolm plays the opening chords on the keyboard, producing a haunting church organ sound. The solemnity of the minor chords continues for a few measures before Malcolm begins to sing. Even though I know it's coming, I startle a little when Malcolm's voice enters my headphones.

That last night, that last time, that last look I can't erase…

It takes everything I have to push away the memory of the first time I heard Malcolm sing these words at Keegan's. I concentrate, instead, on how the song's unfolding now, the sacred, evocative mix created by the sparseness of Malcolm's vocals and the organ. The upright bass joins in on the second verse, its warm *bum, bum, bum* grounding the song as the cello's yearning bleeds slowly into the melody. When the backing vocalists begin to sing, they sound soft and far away, like the voices of children through an open window; they sound like angels. I wipe my palms on my jeans and close my eyes, preparing to join this hymn. I hear the sadness in Malcolm's voice, the hope in my sister's, the heartbeat of the bass. Goose bumps prick my skin. I close my eyes and rub my arms, praying I can give this song my best without coming completely undone. I breathe deep, and when I open my eyes again, I see Liam has turned to face me.

He catches my gaze and winks as if to say *we got this*. We nod at each other as Ricky points to us from the booth, and then we simultaneously crash into the song, Liam with a crunchy guitar chord, me on hi-hat.

One and two and…

One and two and…

One and two and…

I sing the tinkling rhythm to myself as Liam breaks into an uncontrollable grin. Our eyes stay locked and his connection pulls me into the room, into the song, which is crackling with emotion. When we reach the bridge, my foot practically pounds a hole through the kick drum as my arms rain down on the toms and snare.

Bdum, bum, bdum bum, bum…bumbumbumbumbum…bdum, bum, bum, bum…bumbumbumbumbum…

Fear, rage, and grief simmer to the surface, threatening to shatter me like glass. I try to hold it together, try to keep the jagged pieces of my heart from falling to the floor while every note, every word seeps in through the cracks. And yet, I'm playing better than I ever have before, better than I ever will again, maybe. My sister stares at me with a look of wonder, Auntsie smiles through tears, Ricky pumps his fist and mouths *Right on*, and Kiki applauds.

Malcolm's voice rings in my head. *I should have said more, should have done more, found a way to take your place.* The song reaches its climax, we are one solid wall of sound, and then suddenly we all drop out, leaving Malcolm to end where he began, with his vocals and a few haunting chords. I pull off my headphones, and in the quiet, Lynn is with me. I see her as I remember her best, in cutoff shorts, Converse, and a dark blue tank top. She's holding out her arms like she does in my dreams. She wants to help carry this heaviness; instead, I give her this song.

"Fuuucck! That's it! That's gotta be it!" Ricky screams like a little kid in our earphones. "You know how I know? Cause the hair on my arms is standing up."

Everyone rushes to congratulate each other in the main studio, but I snatch my bag off the floor and sneak out the back door. Tears stream down my face, and a sob escapes my throat. Before I know it, I'm running down the hallway toward the elevator. When I hear footsteps behind me, I hide my face, not wanting anyone to see me ugly cry, and frantically push the Down button. When the elevator arrives, I dive inside, place a finger on the first-floor button, and hold it down, willing the doors to close faster. I'm almost in the clear when Malcolm jams his arm between the closing doors and steps inside.

"Cat's Eye." He's breathless.

I wrap my arms around myself and turn away, pissed that he's trapped me like this. That he's seeing me turned inside out.

I'm afraid to give him any more of myself now, knowing that at any moment, he may try to give it back. I wipe my tears with my sleeve and face the wall while I speak.

"I'm not recording that song again. Ever. Whatever it is, it is," I say.

"What it is, is amazing. Don't you want to come back upstairs and hear it? *Please* come back upstairs and hear it. I need to talk to you."

He sounds like my Malcolm, the one I thought I loved, not the one who was willing to push that love aside for getting high. Maybe that's what it means to be broken. There will forever be two sides of one's self with a fault line down the middle. Put two broken people together, and there will come a time when you have a chasm to cross.

The doors open, and I step out into the lobby. Malcolm follows.

"We can talk here," I say.

Malcolm rubs his face with both hands; the blue/black circles under his eyes look painful.

"Look. What happened upstairs. I'm sorry." He takes the pills out of his pocket and hands them back to me. There are only three left. My heart turns cold.

"I never should have asked you to hold these. That was wrong, and I'm sorry."

"You *took* one." I don't hide my outrage.

"I did. I fucked up. And you were right. I couldn't handle

only one. I immediately wanted more. I'm an addict. Addicts take all the pills."

"So why give these to me now?"

"If I screw up again, if something happens to me, I couldn't stand it if you felt responsible."

"Malcolm, I don't want anything to happen to you. I care about you. That's the point."

"I know, I know, and that scares me. Feeling responsible for each other, depending on each other? I'm not ready for that responsibility."

Is he dumping me before we've had a chance to be a couple? The queen of fictitious relationships strikes again.

"So you're saying you don't want me around?" *That you don't want me.*

"I *want* you around. The gig, the band, the tour, it's your choice. But you and I, I think we need to take a step back. Start over as just friends."

"We were never just friends."

"I know. But I'm not good boyfriend material right now. I don't want you putting up with my bullshit. It's not fair to you. I want you to be happy."

"Don't you know I want the same for you?"

Malcolm sighs. "I know you do, Cat's Eye. But I've got a ways to go. I'm sure you've noticed I'm doing a great job of standing in my own fucking way. I don't want to stand in yours too."

He reaches for me, but I scowl and shrug away. He looks hurt. Good.

"What are you saying, Malcolm? Whatever it is, say it."

"I'm saying that letting you go might be the biggest mistake I'll ever make. But not letting you go might be an even bigger one."

I slam the Up button for the elevator, and the doors bing open.

"Go."

He touches my face.

"Go." I say again.

Malcolm backs into the elevator. "You're not leaving?"

I shake my head. "I'll be there in a minute. I want to hear our song."

We both know what a lie sounds like. He looks so desperate and I feel so empty that I almost change my mind before the door closes between us. But I don't want to ruin the post-recording celebration those guys deserve. It's a beautiful thing when people generously give their time and talent in the middle of the night to create a song so perfect and true that it will outlive this goodbye.

TWENTY-NINE

Auntsie finds me alone on the beach, sitting near the water's edge, my arms wrapped around my knees, bare feet in the sand. I'm about twenty feet in front of the overturned lifeguards' chair. Right where I told her I'd be.

"Hey," she says as she plops down next to me.

"Hey."

The boardwalk lights don't reach the onyx waves that stretch for miles and miles toward the dark horizon. I wonder how far I could swim before I got tired. A line from *The Awakening*, the book I was reading when Malcolm walked into my life, pops into my head. *The voice of the sea is seductive, never ceasing, whispering, clamoring, murmuring, inviting the soul to wander in abysses of solitude.* At the time, I had underlined it for its rhythm and musicality more than its meaning.

"Why do I fuck everything up, Auntsie?" I put a protective hand over my cuff bracelet.

"Fuck everything up? What are you talking about? Back there in the studio? You made magic."

"I'm pretty sure Malcolm and I are done."

"Aww, Quinn, babe. I'm sorry. What happened?"

I start to cry. "I caught him going through my stuff. He said he was looking for Advil. But he wanted pills, not Advil, and when I wouldn't give them to him, he said I was acting like his mother. His mother! He said not to save him. I said I was done. I probably shouldn't have said that, but I was so pissed. So I threw the pills at him." I'm talking fast and not making sense.

Auntsie puts her arm around me. "Why don't you calm down and start from the beginning."

I take a deep breath and start with the part about him being a recovering addict. I tell her about the painkillers he asked me to hold for him, and how I was worried about him being on tour alone. I tell her I thought he loved me, and how I thought I loved him too, which is why I decided to go on tour with him.

"Whoa, whoa, whoa. On tour? Painkillers? Why didn't I know about any of this?" Auntsie's pissed. "If our arrangement is going to work, if you really want to live with me when the summer's over, you have to be honest with me. That includes not withholding information."

"I know. I'm sorry. I should have told you. I was going to tell you. But I only decided about the tour last night. It's part of what freaked out Malcolm. I got too close." I scoop up a handful of sand and let the grains slip through my fingers. "Part of me still wants to go. That's crazy, right? Except I know he needs me now more than ever. Even if we are only friends."

"There's a big difference between what he needs and what you want. I told you I'd step in if I saw you making bad decisions. Holding those pills for him without telling me or someone who was more qualified to help him was stupid. Going on the road with him because you want to protect him? Also stupid."

"He warned me about trying to save him."

"Because he knows you can't."

"I love him."

"I know."

"I think he loves me."

"I think he does too. But only as much as he's able to while he fights his demons and tries to find his footing again. That may not be enough for you. It shouldn't be enough for you."

"What am I supposed to do now?" I ask.

Auntsie stands, brushes off the sand, and gazes down the beach. "You know what I love about the ocean?"

"You? Love the ocean?"

"Of course I love the ocean. Would I have spent my whole life three blocks from it if I didn't? It's the *sun* I don't like." Auntsie huffs and takes a deep breath.

"Sorry. Go on," I say. I think maybe I spoiled her moment, but she recovers.

"The ocean changes every day. Tomorrow morning you can walk out here and the surf will look totally different. Sometimes the waves are soft and rolling, other times they're fierce and unforgiving. The winds and the tides are forever reforming and reshaping the landscape. We hear that saying all the time, 'Every day is a new day.' But with the ocean, you can *see* it. It has a way of making you believe the slate really has been wiped clean."

I reach into my pocket and dump the contents of the bag into my hand. Then I push myself up, step toward the crashing waves, and heave the pills as far as I can. I have no idea if they'll dissolve, and I doubt what I've done is environmentally safe, but I don't care. It ends tonight. I never want to see them again.

THIRTY

It's a little past 3:00 a.m. on Sunday morning when we finally pull into Auntsie's driveway.

On the car ride home, my phone buzzed with text after text from Malcolm. I finally turned it off. Evie, amped on adrenaline, talked incessantly for five minutes, then passed out cold. After that, Auntsie let me brood in silence. Thankfully the choir girls took their own car to the studio and left for home from there. I didn't need any outside witnesses to my internal collapse.

Upstairs in my room, I stare out the window. The waxing moon illuminates a watery path to the other side of the bay. What good is light that's borrowed from a star? We have too much in common, the moon and I. I avert my eyes, turn on my phone, and scroll through Malcolm's messages.

Please come back.

I'm standing outside. Where are you?

Cat's Eye? Answer me. You're scaring me.

See you tomorrow?

And finally, about five minutes ago. What you said with "That Last Night"? She heard you. Forgive yourself.

Must be the Vicodin talking.

Bitter as I am, his words still produce the desired effect. They pull on my heart the way the moon does the tides. We may not be together, but we are still trapped in a binary orbit. Only Malcolm and I know what recording that song meant to us. Even after what he said—what we said to each other—I want to hear his voice, to sleep beside him tonight. I clutch my phone and consider it. He and I should have shared that moment in the studio. But he ruined that. I don't know if I'll ever get over what he said to me, or the way he violated my personal space and trust. The more I think about it, the more pissed I get. After all, he already let me go.

I think you should find another drummer, I type. Then I turn off my phone and lay down. My heartbeat sounds like soldiers marching in my ears. I concentrate on counting their steps and emptying my mind. I'm not doing a very good job. When I reach a hundred, I start over again.

I don't remember falling asleep, but I wake up at sunrise. I enjoy a few seconds of peace before last night comes rushing back.

My pillow is damp with a mixture of drool and tears. Perfect. Just perfect. I flip it over and hide my face and consider staying in bed for a year, maybe longer. I wonder if a stunt like that could get me into the *Guinness Book of World Records*. Maybe that would make Mom proud. I imagine the phone call.

"Uh, hey, Mom. You know that life plan we spoke about? I've decided I want to set the world record for lying in bed." Ha! Suddenly, I need to know if my bizarre goal is achievable and who my competition is. I turn on my phone, and my heart twists when I see Malcolm never texted me back. I get the feeling that this is how I'm going to feel for a while, riding a seesaw of emotions as I waver between remembering and forgetting. My bones feel like lead. Which only makes me more determined to stay right where I am.

I breathe deep, then search to see if someone already holds the record for lethargy. Turns out, some guy in a coma in Belgium and an obese man from Kansas City, who had to be forklifted from his bed after three years, might be contenders, though neither has made it into *Guinness* yet.

I don't have three years. I don't have three weeks. Labor Day is fast approaching, and I'm about to become the bird who gets left behind by the flock when it's time to fly south. I pull the covers over my head and block out the sunlight seeping through the blinds. I try to go back to sleep, but can't.

I smell coffee and hear Auntsie shuffling around downstairs

and remember it's Sunday: shelter day. The day I was supposed to be in the studio with Malcolm and Liam as Ricky did the final mix—the last step before the tracks get mastered. The baking of Liam's metaphorical lasagna. After that, the songs are ready for download, or vinyl, or radio, or whatever. Malcolm planned to send the finished audio files to be pressed into compact discs and vinyl records.

The thought of not being part of any of that leaves me hollow. *It's only a band*, I tell myself. A band I bailed on a few hours ago without Malcolm putting up much of a fight. I put the pillow over my head again. Maybe I *can* outlast the man from Kansas City. Maybe I should. I close my eyes tighter and try to think of one good reason to get out of bed. I'm surprised when one pops into my head: *Reggie*. I picture the way he tilts his head so he can study me with his one good eye, his pink tongue lolling from the side of his mouth like a thirsty cartoon dog. There are only two Sundays left in August. Soon, I might not get the chance to see him anymore. Having failed at coming up with my own life plan, it's doubtful Mom will let me stay with Auntsie. Who will give him baths? Take him on long walks?

I fling one leg out from under the covers and force it toward the floor. My body eventually follows. Twenty minutes later, showered and dressed, I arrive in the kitchen. Auntsie's standing at the counter, smearing a gluten-free English muffin with SunButter.

"I think we should adopt Reggie." My words stop Auntsie mid-smear. I don't know how this figures into my life plan, but at this moment, it's what I've got.

She doesn't speak, only stares at some point on the wall as she licks the end of the butter knife.

Finally, she says, "Okay then." She's nodding slowly like she's listening to a song only she can hear. "Let's go make that furry guy ours."

At first, it's a normal shelter visit with Reggie. I brush him, play ball with him, take him for an extra long walk, during which I give him ample time to absorb his surroundings with his nose as he selects the perfect spot to do his business. When he's finished, he kicks up dirt with his back paws and makes an agitated grunting noise, like his poop has wronged him in some way. Reggie can be very dramatic.

When we're done with our walk, Reggie and I meet up with Auntsie, who has been inside filling out the necessary paperwork to bring Reggie home with us. We'll be foster parents for a few weeks until the adoption is final.

"That's it!" Ben says when she's through. "We'll miss our Reggie, but you're going to make him very happy."

When I carry Reggie out the door instead of back to his kennel, he cocks his head as if to say, "Uh, Quinn? Where're we going?" When he sees Auntsie's car, he begins to shiver. I can't be sure if he's nervous—maybe car rides equal bad news to shelter dogs?—or happy. Maybe his inner Chihuahua is getting the better of him. Those little dogs are known to be shakers.

Once we're in the passenger seat and buckled in, he immediately climbs up toward my shoulder, tucks himself under my chin, and continues to shake while licking my face.

"It's okay, Reg. We're taking you home," I say. "You'll like it there. I know I do."

"Then you should probably stay," Auntsie says, glancing sideways. "Reggie's going to need you in the fall. I think your mom would understand that."

"She'd understand college more."

"True. But a dog's a good start."

"A dog's not really a good start."

"Maybe not," Auntsie acknowledges. "But I had to say something."

THIRTY-ONE

Back at Auntsie's, Evie's sitting in the living room sipping coffee when Reggie bursts onto the scene. He skids like a cartoon character as he tries to gain traction on the hardwood floors, but once he hits the area rug, he finds his footing and starts doing fast loops around the couch. He yips and wags his tail as he makes circle after circle. The three of us go cross-eyed trying to take in the rocketing brown blur.

"He's the cutest, ugliest dog I've ever seen," Evie squeals.

"I know, right?" I say.

"Hey, maybe we can enter him in one of those contests," Auntsie muses.

"And exploit his unique appearance? No way!" I say.

We're so caught up in Reggie's euphoria that no one notices

Liam and Kiki knocking on the screen door. When they call out their hellos, I scoop up Reggie and walk toward them.

"Q! What up? Is that a dog?" Liam cups his eyes and presses his face against the screen.

"Liam, Keeks. What are you guys doing here?" Reggie and I step outside. The noon sun is beating down, heating up the thick, humid air.

Liam holds up a CD and waves it back and forth like he's the queen of England.

"What's that?" I ask.

"Rough mix. Ricky wants you to listen and let him know if there's anything you want fixed."

"Why me? They're Malcolm's songs."

"Malcolm's already listened to them. He's been there all night with Ricky. They need fresh ears. Or maybe they need someone fresh. Either way, it's you."

I ignore Liam's attempt to get a rise out of me and take heart in the fact that Malcolm was at the studio and didn't sleep at home last night. I don't trust Malcolm alone with himself. I take the CD from Liam.

"Thanks."

"Ricky says the speakers in the studio are too perfect. You need to listen to the rough mix in the wild to get a true sense of what the songs sound like. Listen in the car with us. We're heading back to the studio."

Reggie licks my face. I try to see around his furry head.

"Yeah, about that. I'm sort of done."

Liam holds up his hand. "I already know you tried bailing. Uh-uh. No way. Not going to let you do that."

"I'm sorry, Liam," I say. "You guys need to find another drummer."

"Malcolm doesn't want to find another drummer, and neither do I. We need you for the Labor Day weekend gig. Plus, get this: Ricky thinks Malcolm should take a full band on the road. He says a solo acoustic tour won't do the songs justice. Won't sell CDs and download cards."

Kiki, who's been uncharacteristically quiet, moves closer and pets Reggie between his ears. He's been tilting his head back and forth like he's listening to our conversation and understands.

"He asked Liam to go with him," she says softly. I can see the worry in her eyes. I don't blame her.

My head whips toward Liam and I narrow my eyes.

"What about college? You're supposed to start in, like, three weeks. You told him no, right?"

Kiki's grimace tells me he hasn't. College girls are one thing—groupies are another story.

"Travis is going," Liam says.

"Well, good for Travis." Though I have to admit, after watching him casually hand Malcolm a beer, it might be better if Liam came along on the tour. But that would be selfish. Come September, there's only one place Liam should be.

"Travis can play bass, Malcolm can keep on playing guitar, and you can start Rutgers like you're supposed to."

"Thank you," Kiki mouths.

"But it's only a few months! I can start college in January. This is a once-in-a-lifetime opportunity. Plus, not to brag or anything, but…" Liam begins.

Kiki rolls her eyes. "We all know you're the better guitarist, babe."

"So what did you tell Malcolm?" I ask Liam.

"I told him I would think about it. You should too."

Kiki and I exchange a look. She knows I have already thought about it. But what she doesn't know is that my telling Malcolm I wanted to go on tour with him triggered the implosion of our not-quite-real relationship.

Reggie barks, as if on cue.

"Reggie thinks I should stay."

"You're taking advice from a weird-looking squirrel now, Q?"

"He needs me," I say.

"So does Malcolm. So do I," Liam argues. "Come to the studio with us."

I shake my head. "I can't. Not today. But I'll think about the other stuff. The gig, the tour."

"You will?" Liam's pleased.

"Sure." I'm worn out. I want this conversation to be over with. I want Liam to leave. I want to be alone.

Kiki hugs me before they leave.

"Malcolm was devastated last night when you didn't come back," she whispers in my ear. "He said to tell you the stress of being in the studio got to him. He wants you there today."

"Tell him I need some time alone."

THIRTY-TWO

An hour later, I get my wish. Auntsie announces that she's taking Evie back to North Jersey.

"Do you wanna take a ride?" she asks.

"No, I'll stay here with Reggie," I say.

On her way out the door, Evie hugs me tighter and longer than she has in years, thanking me for the experience of recording and saying she hopes things with Malcolm work themselves out.

"Don't worry," she says. "As far as Mom's concerned, I will tell her everything's peachy."

Peachy?

"Don't say peachy. It'll make her suspicious. What would Ricky say?"

Evie makes the peace sign. "Righteous. I'll tell her things

are righteous," she says, laughing. "Ricky was the best. See you in a week."

That's right—Evie, Ashley, Kate, and Mom are spending the final week of summer here, which means Mom's going to want her room back and I'll be sleeping on the couch with Reggie. I watch him sleeping there now, his tiny chest rising and falling. That won't be so bad.

After they leave, I'm seized with a sudden restlessness. It's a beautiful day, but my mood doesn't match the sunny weather. So, I close all the blinds to make the bungalow as dark as possible, then go upstairs to retrieve my electronic drum kit. Once it's set up on the coffee table, I browse through Auntsie's vinyl collection, looking for the right music to work out the knot in my chest that's making it hard to breathe.

I start with the A's and assemble a stack of albums that could easily be labeled "Malcolm and Quinn: The Greatest Hits." AC/DC, The Beatles, The White Stripes, The Sundays, and the song Malcolm played during his sound check at Keegan's—"I'll Be You" by The Replacements. I'm in the mood to throw salt in my wounds before I lick them. In my quest to torture myself, I discover Amy Winehouse, her beautifully jazzy voice, genius lyrics, musical arrangements that sound like '50s music. She's like Adele with no hope. I work my way through my set list of pain, playing along when I can and making shit up when I can't. I just want to hit hard and play loud. Oddly, Reggie sleeps through most of it.

When I'm done, I toss my sticks on top of my crappy electronic drums and collapse beside Reggie on the couch. He readjusts himself, turning in circles, before curling up at my feet and tucking his nose against his belly.

I turn on the TV and spend the next twenty minutes watching an infomercial about a mega juicer. I have to say, these people almost, *almost*, have me convinced that the green sludge they're chugging down tastes delicious.

"Ugh, what the hell am I doing, Reggie?" He opens his working eye, then lets it fall closed again.

Time passes by so slowly, each second punctuated by the ticking brass clock on the wall. It's hard to keep my mind from imagining what's going on in the studio without me while simultaneously fighting the urge to check up on Malcolm. I need to know if he's okay, but don't want to risk inviting another comparison to his mother.

Then there's the matter of really, really wanting to have a say in the final mix of the songs. But to do that, I have to listen to them. But where? The speaker on my laptop is crappy, and Auntsie, the vinyl queen, doesn't own a CD player. I could take Reggie for a ride in the car; maybe even drive over the bridge to Keegan's and get a second listen of the songs there. But that might be too much for Reggie. He didn't do so well the last time he was in a car, and I don't want to lock him in his crate and leave him alone. Not on his first day here.

That's when I remember there's another option, one that's a lot closer to home. I shuffle my feet gently and rouse the little guy.

"Come on, Reggie. Shake the sleep off those paws. We're taking a walk."

THIRTY-THREE

Aaron, my boss at the Ben Franklin, is surprised when he looks up and sees me standing there with a dog in one hand and a CD in the other.

"Quinn! Is that a dog?"

Why do people keep asking that? Reggie barks as if to say, *What do you think, Einstein?*

Aaron is in his "office," a converted supply closet adjacent to the beach chair aisle, writing out checks.

"This is Reggie. We adopted him this morning, and I didn't want to leave him home alone."

Aaron understands. He treats his ninety-pound Rottweiler like a furry child.

He takes a clipboard off the wall and starts flipping through pages.

"Are you on the schedule today?"

I laugh because he thinks I showed up to work with a dog, and he's still okay with it. I love this place.

"Oh no, I'm not working today. I'm here to ask a favor." I show him the CD and explain. Five minutes later, Reggie and I are sitting in side-by-side beach chairs in the back of the store, listening as Malcolm's songs play on the store sound system. At my request, the music is turned up louder than the store's usual summer play mix of Jack Johnson, Sinatra, The Beach Boys, and Bob Marley.

I recline in my chair like I'm sunning myself and close my eyes, trying to take in the songs as a whole, but I'm also making mental notes about the tracks I want to listen to again and things that need to change—the guitar levels on track two, the vocals on tracks one and two, the guitar on track three. Track four's also too "bright" with too much high end, not enough bass. When the opening chords of track five, "That Last Night," begin to play, I scoop up Reggie and sit him in my lap. I need a paw to hold. Tourists pass by clutching souvenir T-shirts and mugs, two kids twirl the postcard rack, and Aaron helps a customer get a boogie board down from the top shelf. All of this goes on around me while the darkest parts of my soul pour out of the overhead speakers without causing so much as a moment's interruption in this ordinary summer day.

At home, I make sure all my notes are in order before calling Ricky.

"Quinn Gallo!" he yells when he hears my voice. "We've been waiting on you, girl. Here, let me put you on speaker."

Great. So much for my plan to ask him not to mention it's me.

"Hey y'all, say 'hey' to Quinn," Ricky says, sounding farther away now that he's on speaker.

In the background, I hear Liam say, "Hey, Q," and Kiki say, "Hey, Quinny!" I think I hear another male voice say my name, but I'm not sure if it's Malcolm or Travis.

"Tell us what you got, Quinn," Ricky says.

I give them my notes for changes, track by track, and I'm pleased when I hear Ricky acknowledging what I'm saying, and in many cases, validating my choices and opinions. Thankfully, when I'm finished, he takes me off speakerphone.

"You have a great ear, girl," he says. "You ever think about doing this for a livin'?"

I've never thought about doing *anything* for a living.

"Me? A recording engineer?"

"Hells yeah," Ricky says. "I don't exactly see you as a touring musician, but I think you'd be amazing behind the scenes. Think about it. After this project wraps up, I'd be happy to talk your ear off about this crazy business."

It's hard to picture adult Quinn, arriving at work every day, being in charge of something big like producing an album. And yet, that's what I am, right? An adult. Legally, at least. Next month, when I turn nineteen, I'll have been one for a whole year.

"Wow, Ricky. Thank you. So I can call you?"

"Anytime, Quinn Gallo. Anytime. You've got my card."

According to Ricky, a professional drummer I am not. I kind of knew that. But I have a bright future in sound. Ha! Yeah, right. I'd like to say I'm going to get on that, but after I hang up, all I can think about is Malcolm. Was he in the room when I called? Did he leave when he heard my voice? Is he angry? I should have handled the situation better. He didn't know the narcotic prescribed to ease the pain in his hand would also ease the pain in his life—that he'd become addicted. I caught Malcolm having a weak moment, like that time he showed up drunk on the boardwalk. Only this time instead of trying to help, I pounced on him. Then I followed that by telling him to find another drummer. Why?

Because he pushed my love away.

That's it, isn't it? And the worst part is, I let him.

Around ten that night, Auntsie finds me pretty much how she left me: on the couch. Reggie is asleep at my feet and the Weather Channel is on, looping that same fragment of a tune over and over again. My "drums," two mugs, the albums I failed to reshelve, and an empty box of cereal—the remains of my lunch and dinner—are on the coffee table, along with the two books from Auntsie's reading list that I opened, then abandoned (*To the Lighthouse* and *Written on the Body*).

Auntsie takes in the mess. "Amy Winehouse? Oh boy. I'd ask how your day went, but that says it all right there," she says.

"'Tears Dry on Their Own' and 'Addicted' really speak to me," I say. I've been listening to "Wake up Alone" too, but I don't want to bring up my absent nights.

Auntsie tickles Reggie between the ears and rouses him. He didn't notice her come in, but considering he was able to sleep through my drumming, I'm not surprised. It's possible "deafness" can be added to his list of conditions.

He gets all excited when he sees Auntsie. He leaps from the couch and dances on his hind legs in front of her, pawing at her knees. His yap sounds like he's saying, "Hello, hello, hello." Auntsie bends down and picks him up. Holding him at arm's length, she looks him in the eye.

"Seems like someone has made himself right at home." She turns to me. "Not sure how we'll get him in the crate tonight."

"I miss my drums," I say, ignoring her comment about Reggie and his crate.

"Stop trying to change the subject. You've already turned our shelter dog into a pampered couch potato." With Reggie tucked in the crook of one arm, Auntsie motions for me to move my feet and sits down. Her eyes pan from my electronic kit to the space briefly inhabited by the real deal.

"Technically, the drums were never yours, Quinn baby. You were borrowing them. And they never spent much time here anyway."

I nod, accepting my dose of tough love, then grab a pillow and hug it to my chest. "If they'd been my drums, they would have been the green sparkle kind anyway. Green sparkle drums are awesome."

Auntsie pats my legs. "I'll give you one more day of sad songs and wallowing. After that, it's time to take the advice of Robert Frost."

Do I even want to ask? I don't have to. Auntsie's already giving advice from the great American poet.

"Get up. Make your bed. And make up your mind about what kind of day it's going to be."

Leave it to some dead laureate to put a crimp in my plan to pursue glory on the pages of the *Guinness Book of World Records.*

"You never got to play cowbell," I lament. "Remember? Malcolm said you could play cowbell."

Auntsie squints at me. "Are we having the same conversation here? Have you been drinking?"

"What?! No." I haven't touched alcohol since my ill-fated evening with Mr. G. Sheesh. She was the one who wanted to play cowbell.

She looks at me sideways. "Just checking. Why don't you walk Reggie? I'll bring his crate up to your room, though I have the feeling it will go unused."

"My room?"

"Yep. I've got to be at work early tomorrow. I'll leave the matter of how and where he sleeps to you. Plus, you look like you could use the company."

"How's Mom?" I ask as I push myself off the couch and search for Reggie's retractable leash. Auntsie stayed at my mom's house and had dinner with Mom and Evie.

"She's good. Looking forward to spending some time down here next week. Evie told her all about the recording session."

"She did? What did Mom say?" I bend down and hook Reggie's leash to his harness, trying to act like I don't care about Auntsie's answer.

"She was genuinely interested in the whole process. It was hard not to be. Evie was still riding a high."

Of course. I'm sure it was Evie's role in the process, not mine, that had her so intrigued. Immediately, I feel guilty for thinking that way. I can't blame Mom if Evie's her favorite. My straight-arrow sister has never given Mom one day's trouble. But me? I'm not so easy to love, I get that, but I *have* tried super hard to not give Mom an ulcer or more gray hairs. After Lynn's accident, and again after the scandal with my teacher, I attempted to tiptoe through life, fade into the background, not get in Mom's way. But I did it with about as much grace as a giraffe on ice skates.

Worse though, I caused Mom to lose the friend she had in Lynn's mom. They used to take walks together, were in the same book club, took turns driving Lynn and I places. After the accident, they didn't have daughters the same age anymore. Lynn's family moved a few towns away the year after she died, and even though I felt guilty about it—because I'd caused that too, hadn't I?—I was relieved. I'd kept waiting in silent terror for them to ask me what really happened that day. If someone had asked, I would have told him or her that it was my bad idea to bike Mount Doom. But after they moved, I realized no one ever would. I shouldn't have gotten off that easy.

It's time to forgive yourself, Malcolm's text said. I honestly don't think I ever will, but maybe I should start by saying I'm sorry.

"I should call Mom tomorrow," I say.

"I know she'd love to hear from you."

In the years since Lynn's death, I've accepted the life I've been dealt, welcoming it as a silent atonement for what I did. But I haven't faced it, have I? I've never owned it. Never sat among support group members and announced my sins like Malcolm did. That moment in Keegan's parking lot with Malcolm when I blurted out what I'd done, it was like breaking the airtight seal on the grief I've carried around with me all this time. And I've let some of the secrets and hurt spill out, but now it's time to really own it.

I'm surprised when Auntsie speaks again. I'd forgotten she was here.

"I have the day off Wednesday. We should do something together. Something fun."

"I want to visit the cemetery," I say.

Auntsie nods slowly. "Okaaay. I was thinking Six Flags or a day trip to New York, but that works too."

I'm not quite ready for fun, but I'm getting there.

THIRTY-FOUR

It snowed on the morning they buried Lynn, big cotton-like flakes that melted as soon as they hit the ground, like the earth was swallowing all its beauty.

Winter took its last gasp that day. Much like summer is doing now. August's heavy breath presses down on Auntsie and I, making me wish I wore a hat and sunscreen. Silently, we make our way to Lynn's grave while the crickets, cicadas, and katydids sing a discordant song, their volume peaking with urgency every few seconds before it repeats all over again. Reggie trots beside us as we make our way between the rows of headstones, his jaunty steps offering a lightness to our heavy ones. He seems content to be surrounded by so much grass.

"You sure you don't want to do this alone?" Auntsie says. "I can wait in the car."

"I'm sure I can't do this alone."

I spent yesterday prepping to take the one-hour drive to the place where I said my final goodbye to Lynn three years ago. Or more like the place I was *supposed* to say my final goodbye. I don't recall uttering a single word that day. Except for the snow, I don't remember much. I'm trying to remember it now, but I can't. What color was the coffin? Did I place a flower on the grave? Mostly I remember not wanting to be seen. As if all it would take was one glance for everyone to realize what I'd done.

In my hands I carry a bouquet of sunflowers. Tucked between the stems are a copy of the rough mix of "That Last Night" and a letter I wrote to Lynn. When we find the spot, I bend down and lay the bouquet in the shadow created by the stone angel who sits atop the headstone with her open wings and downcast eyes, keeping watch over my best friend.

I know Lynn will never read the letter, which is five pages, single-spaced. But I needed a place to put all my thoughts, and I want her to have them. I have hopes that somehow, wherever she is, she heard the song on Sunday and knew it was meant for her. Still, I'm not leaving that second part to chance. I reach into my bag and pull out a portable speaker, then cue up the song on my phone while Auntsie spreads a blanket. She barely has a chance to straighten it before Reggie hurls himself into the middle. Silly little dog. Auntsie and I sit on either side of him. He waits for us to get comfortable then he lays his chin on Auntsie's knee.

"Ready?" I pose the question more to myself than Auntsie.

"Light it up," she says, imitating Ricky. I get the feeling that the Ricky imitations are going to last around our house.

I stare at Lynn's headstone, at the dates bookending her too-short time on earth. I consider announcing myself, letting her know I'm here. But in the end, I do the only thing that seems to make any sense and hit Play.

When the song is over, Auntsie grabs my hand and gives it a squeeze. I can't look at her.

"Lynn died because of me." I say those words with conviction and ownership.

"What?! No she didn't, Quinn baby. She was hit by a car. It was an accident."

"An accident I caused. I raced across the intersection that day. She was following me. I made her think it was safe, and she trusted me. It's my fault she's gone."

"Nobody blames you. It could have easily been you."

"It should have been me. I wish it had been me. I made a big mistake, and Lynn paid for it."

I'm twisting my bracelet back and forth, making my wrist red. Auntsie puts her hand on top of mine to still it.

"Don't, Quinn. Just don't. After the accident...we thought

we were going to lose you too. You were traumatized and retreated so far into yourself… No one knew how to reach you. It was like all the light was gone from your eyes. But I had no idea you blamed yourself."

"Everyone blamed me."

"Aww, Quinn. You're wrong. So wrong. It's time to forgive yourself."

"I don't know if I can."

"I get that. I totally do. But until you forgive yourself, you won't love yourself."

Love myself? I can barely peacefully coexist with myself.

I'm shaking my head. "I can't."

"You have to. If you don't decide you're worth every good thing this world has to offer, you're going to stay stuck. Believe me, I know all about Stucksville. I lived there for quite a while."

"When did you finally blow out of that town?"

Auntsie scoops up Reggie and kisses him on the head. "About a week ago. Don't wait as long as me."

THIRTY-FIVE

On our way home from North Jersey and the cemetery, Auntsie makes a detour off the Garden State Parkway.

"Why are we exiting here?" I ask.

"It's a surprise. You'll see."

Twenty minutes later, we're pulling into the parking lot of a Sam Ash music store.

"Come on, let's go in."

"What? Why?" I look down at Reggie sleeping on my lap. "What about him?"

"Hand him to me. I got this."

As we walk through the front door, we're stopped by store security.

"No pets allowed," says a burly guy dressed in all black like a bouncer.

Auntsie smiles. "He's a rescue dog who needs to be socialized," she says. "We were told to expose him to a variety of people and environments."

The security dude, Phil, according to his name tag, looks dubious.

"Like music stores?"

"Exactly, Phil," Auntsie says.

Phil's not buying it, but he still waves us in. "Fine. As long as you hold him. If he pees on the floor, he's out of here."

Bet he doesn't get to say that every day.

Auntsie salutes him with her free hand. "Can you point me toward the drums?"

"Left at the guitars. The drum room is in the back of the store."

"Thanks, Phil. Come on, Quinn baby."

I smile at Phil and follow Auntsie, who walks through the store like she comes here every day with a one-eyed, toothless Chihuahua mix. I look around, surprised at the number of people who are here at lunchtime on a Wednesday.

"Don't these people have jobs?" I ask.

"Musicians," Auntsie answers.

"Right."

We reach the drum room, and Auntsie makes a beeline for a

red sparkle set that's sitting on a low platform. She steps up onto the riser with Reggie still in tow, sits on the stool, and begins to pump the kick drum pedal. The *thump, thump, thump* summons a sales associate sporting funky glasses and a long ponytail. He looks confused. I'm guessing it's because of the dog.

"Uh, can I help you?"

"You sure can, Mike." Auntsie's very good at paying attention to name tags. "My niece would like to take these for a spin. Would you have some sticks she can borrow?"

"Sure thing. I'll get you some."

I'm shaking my head as we watch him retreat to find drumsticks. "Auntsie, what are you doing? I don't want to play drums right now."

"You have to."

"Why?"

"Because I want to be sure you like them before I buy them."

"Auntsie, I can't let you do that. They're too expensive and—" I'm about to say that I'm not in a band anymore when Mike returns and hands me the sticks.

"Here ya go. Cool glasses, by the way."

"Back at you."

Auntsie vacates the seat and motions for me to sit. I was kind of hoping Mike would leave, but no. He's in this for the long haul. He crosses his arms over his chest and settles in for the Quinn Show. This is so embarrassing. Drummers usually get to hide behind the band. Here, on the riser, under the fluorescent lights of Sam Ash, I *am* the band. I make myself as comfortable as I can under the circumstances and begin playing a simple groove—a groove I'm certain I won't screw up.

I'm holding my own when Mike calls out, "Try a roll!"

"Hey, Mike," I hear Auntsie say. "Do these come in green?"

"They do. Let me check our inventory to see if we have them in stock."

When Mike's out of sight, I get fancier, playing some of the more complicated drum parts I worked out for Malcolm's songs. I'm really getting into it when my phone buzzes with a text. I can't help it. I stop to check it. It's been four days since I've seen or spoken to Malcolm. His silence is burning a hole in my stomach. I glance at my phone. It's Liam. CALL ME!

The exclamation point and all caps give me a heart arrhythmia.

"Q!" He sounds breathless when he answers the phone, and I panic.

"What's wrong? Is Malcolm all right?"

"Geez, Q. It's like you have an Italian mother's sixth sense. He's fine. I'm fine too, by the way."

I feel like a jerk. "Liam, I'm sorry I—"

"Yeah, yeah, save it, Q. We've got a huge problem."

I grip my drumsticks tighter. "Problem?"

"Malcolm's auditioning drummers on Saturday."

I'm being replaced? The irony of finding out this news while I'm surrounded by drums is not lost on me. So much for leaving the decision about the Keegan's gig and the tour up to me. Just friends. Just nothing, Malcolm meant. I try to play it cool.

"Well, it makes sense. I quit the band. He needs a drummer."

"Un-quit. Come to practice tomorrow night."

They're practicing without me?

"Who's playing drums?"

"Malcolm's going to play drums while Travis learns the bass parts."

"Sounds like you've got everything under control."

"Q, we need you there."

"Malcolm doesn't seem to think so. Look, if he wants to audition drummers, I'm not going to stop him. I was considering playing with you guys at the Keegan's gig, but the tour—" I break off because even though I'm hurt and pissed, I know Malcolm's right to move on. I don't know what I want and I can't expect him to sit around waiting for me to decide. He leaves in two weeks. "He should replace me."

"You're irreplaceable, Q. Malcolm knows that."

When did Liam get so sweet?

"Thanks for saying that, but we both know there are much, much better drummers out there."

"Maybe, but there's only one Q. Come to practice tomorrow night."

I miss our power trio. I really do. But the magic the three of us had is already gone. The addition of Travis changed our dynamic. And yet, I know in my heart that Travis has more of a right to be part of Malcolm's next band than I do. They shared the same dream once. They probably still do.

"I don't know."

"Yes, you do, Q. I'm going to tell Malcolm to call you." Liam hangs up.

Auntsie gives me a side squeeze as I step down off the drum platform. "Sounds like Malcolm's taking care of Malcolm. Might be time for Quinn to take care of Quinn."

Mike returns before I can answer.

"We don't have the green in stock, but if you order them today, we can have them shipped to your house for free."

"I don't think—" I begin.

But Auntsie cuts me off by handing me Reggie.

"Hold the dog, please." Then she reaches into her bag, whips out a credit card, and gives it to Mike. "We'll take them."

THIRTY-SIX

I'm a drummer with drums, but no band.

That's what I'm thinking as we merge back onto the Garden State Parkway toward the shore. I know I won't be showing up for practice tomorrow night. Not without hearing from Malcolm first. It would be too awkward.

"Auntsie?"

"Hmm?"

"Thanks again for the drums. I love them, but you didn't have to do that. They were so expensive."

"I wanted to. Consider it your birthday present and Christmas present."

I laugh. "For the next two years, you mean? And you're okay with me setting them up in the living room?"

"Yup. They can stay there for as long as they want."

"I'm pretty sure they want to stay through the fall, maybe longer."

"Fine with me, but they should probably discuss that with your mom."

We're crossing the Driscoll Bridge, "The Big Bridge," as we used to call it when Mom drove us from North Jersey to the shore. It spans the Raritan River and marks the halfway point in our trip.

"Auntsie? Do you mind making some additional stops on the way home?"

"How many is *additional*?"

"Two. Possibly three, if we're feeling ambitious."

"The destinations will determine my level of ambition."

"Well, one of those stops definitely needs to be food. I'm starving," I say.

"A fish taco would definitely incent me. What are the other two stops?"

"Monmouth University and Ocean County College."

She raises her eyebrows. "Cemeteries and colleges? Next time I have a day off, I'm so picking our destinations."

"At least I didn't drag you to a Narcan training session. That's where I'm going tomorrow."

"Seriously?"

I nod. "The health department is hosting it."

Auntsie shakes her head in a way that says *I'm not touching that topic now.* "I was teasing about the colleges. I'm actually thrilled to hear you're thinking about college."

"Don't get too excited yet. I'm only tossing around some ideas here." I tell her about my phone call with Ricky and how it got me thinking. "Monmouth has an audio engineering program, but it's super expensive, and I'm not sure I'm ready to commit. I thought I might ease into the whole college thing with a couple community college classes in the fall."

"Why didn't you tell me sooner? This is exciting." She puts on her blinker to exit the highway. "Okay then. Pee stop for Reggie, fish tacos for us, then on to the colleges."

"Sounds like a plan," I say.

"Feels good, doesn't it?"

"I hate to admit that Mom could be right, but yes. Yes, it does."

My whirlwind of college tours with Auntsie and Reggie helps me forget about Malcolm and the cold reality that he's moving on without me. At times, especially while Auntsie's reliving her glory days at Rutgers, I don't even think about how much it hurts that I haven't heard from him. Liam said he was going to tell Malcolm to call me. Did he? Will Malcolm listen? He didn't have any trouble listening when I told Kiki to tell him I needed space.

By the time we leave Ocean County College, poor Reggie

is exhausted. He's actually snoring in the back seat. We take him home, feed him, and leave him sleeping comfortably on the couch. So much for setting limits.

That night, Auntsie and I walk along the boardwalk, eating blue cotton candy. The sun is setting on what seems like a very long day. It's like I ran an emotional marathon. I'm both energized and nervous by the thought of taking college classes, and unsure if I want to remain a bandless drummer.

"Liam wants me to go to practice tomorrow night. He thinks I should play the Keegan's gig and go on tour."

"What do you want to do?" Auntsie asks.

I pluck off a big chunk of cotton candy and let it dissolve on my tongue. "It's hard. I'm worried about Malcolm being on tour. Travis has already challenged his sobriety. What kind of friend hands a recovering addict a beer? I feel like I should go, even if we are only friends. Even if I'm not the drummer. Someone needs to have Malcolm's back."

"You didn't answer my question. What do *you* want to do?"

I can't answer that without knowing what Malcolm *wants* me to do. But I know that's not what Auntsie want to hear.

I shrug. "Today has given me a lot to think about."

"It certainly has."

We walk out to the edge of the ride pier and watch two kids tethered to a cable get hoisted two hundred feet into the air and hurled out over the dark ocean like a human slingshot.

"I have a feeling if I ever did that, it would be the last thing I ever did. They'd have to use the defibrillator on me," Auntsie says.

"Come on, let's go to the free fall tower."

"That's more my speed."

After handing over our tickets, we kick off our flips-flops at the base of the tower and harness ourselves into our seats. We wait for the ride attendant to do a final safety check before she gives the all clear. This is the moment that makes me feel like I need to pee. The ride's hydraulics make a loud *chuuush* and we're whisked to top of the hundred-fifty-foot tower. My heart pounds while we're held in place, anticipating the drop. I take in as much as I can: the boardwalk's neon glow, the waves crashing for miles along the shore...and then *bam*! I'm falling. Auntsie and I scream the whole way down. When we hit the bottom, the thrill of the fall is immediately replaced by the melancholy of falling back to earth. Gravity. It gets us every time.

THIRTY-SEVEN

I stay glued to my phone while getting ready for my shift at the Ben Franklin, bringing it everywhere, including the bathroom while I shower. I keep hoping Malcolm will call or text to tell me about the drummer auditions, to ask me to reconsider practice tonight, to tell me he misses me. I'd also be okay with him saying he never wants to see me again. Sad, crushed, but okay. It's the not knowing that's killing me.

I'm rinsing the conditioner from my hair when I hear my ringtone. I rush out of the shower. With water dripping into my eyes and no glasses, I can't make out the caller ID. I pick up.

"Malcolm?"

There's a long pause before a woman who isn't Malcolm speaks.

"Is this Quinn?"

Her voice is vaguely familiar, but I can't place it.

"Yes, this is Quinn."

"You sound so grown up."

"Um, who is this?"

"Sorry, hon. This is Mrs. Sullivan, Lynn's mom."

I wrap myself in a towel and sink down onto the edge of the tub, dizzy. The shower steam, poor ventilation, and the lump in my throat are preventing any oxygen from getting to my brain.

"Quinn, are you there?"

"Yes, yes. I'm here. Sorry. Hello. How are you?"

"I'm okay, hon. How are you? Your mom tells me you're living with your aunt this summer. I called her for your phone number. I hope you don't mind."

"Mind? No, of course not." I forgot how, like my mom, Lynn's mom used to call everyone "hon." *Do you want some more milk, hon? Did you want to stay for dinner, hon?* How can she still stand to call me that after all that's happened?

"We were at the cemetery yesterday, visiting Lynn. We must have missed you by a few hours. The lovely flowers you left were still fresh."

It takes me a few minutes to process that Lynn's family and I visited her grave on the same day. I open the bathroom door, let in the fresh air, and breathe deep.

"Again, I hope you don't mind, hon, but we read the letter

you wrote to Lynn. After reading it, I knew I had to reach out. I had to clarify something. Those days and weeks that followed her death were very dark for all of us. I think maybe you didn't get all the information, or maybe you don't remember. The person in the SUV that killed Lynn was texting while driving. Not only that, but she also ran a red light. There were witnesses. She was looking at her phone at the time of the impact. She never hit her brakes. She never even saw our Lynn. If she'd looked up… If she'd hit her brakes… But that's not what happened."

"Or if we'd gone to the library that day like Lynn wanted to," I say in a voice just above a whisper. "Or if she hadn't followed me across that busy street."

"Quinn, listen to me. If there's one thing I've learned after losing Lynn, it's that the 'what ifs' will kill you. You are not responsible for what happened to Lynn. After reading your letter, I couldn't let you live another day thinking that you were."

She's being far too generous. I'm having a hard time believing that I deserve this reprieve. I'm comfortable with my guilt. I wear it like a scratchy, wool scarf in all kinds of weather.

"Mrs. Sullivan, what I wrote in that letter, I should have said those words to you too. I'm sorry. I'm so, so sorry."

"I know you are, honey. And I'm sorry you've spent all this time blaming yourself, but I want you to know we never did. Lynn wouldn't have wanted that. She loved you. You were her best friend."

I bite the inside of my cheek to keep from crying. "Thank you, Mrs. Sullivan. Thank you for saying all this."

"I'm happy we found your letter and that timing…fate, maybe…brought us back together."

"It wasn't fate. It was Lynn."

It takes her a few seconds to respond, and when she does, I can tell she's crying.

"Take care of yourself, Quinn. I told your mom that next time we're in town, we should all get together."

"I'd like that."

"Oh, and one more thing before I hang up. Your song? It's beautiful. You have a gift, hon. I hope you use it."

Sometimes the ocean wipes the slate clean. Other times, it's a phone call. And the power of forgiveness.

I sit there, frozen, in my towel for a long time as Mrs. Sullivan's words slowly penetrate the portion of my brain where this tragedy has lived like a parasite, eating away at my life. When I finally move, my hair is almost dry. I walk to my room. My limbs are lighter, like the anchor that held me down for so long has finally broken free. I could run five miles if I wanted to. I don't want to, but it's amazing to feel like I could. I grab my cell and dial the one person I need to talk to right now.

"Lynn's mother called."

"Tell me everything."

"It could take a while," I say.

"That's okay. I've always got time for you, hon." Although it isn't always easy to tell with Mom, I think I hear her smiling through the phone.

"I'm sorry."

"For what?" Mom sounds genuinely surprised.

"For being a screwup. For the way my screwups affected and embarrassed you. I'm sorry if I let you down. I know I'm a disappointment."

"Quinn, listen to me. You've never been a disappointment. I'm proud of you. *I'm* sorry I never knew you felt responsible for Lynn's accident. Until I talked to Mrs. Sullivan yesterday, I had no idea *how* you felt. You've been living alone with a hurt you should have shared. After the accident…" There are tears in her voice. "I couldn't reach you. I knew you were hurting and it broke my heart. All I've ever wanted is for you to be happy. I worried about the choices you were making. You seemed determined to hurt yourself."

"I was. But I'm not anymore."

"Good. That's good to hear." Neither of us says anything for a few moments and then Mom begins talking again.

"You know, I wasn't going to tell you this, but I went to see that band teacher of yours."

The air rushes out of my lungs. "What? When?"

"Right after you left for the shore. I wanted him to know that the blame for what happened fell squarely on him. I also told him to stay away from you—and all his future students if he knows what's good for him. I may have called him a pervert."

I can tell she's proud of herself for that last part. It makes me smile a little.

"What'd he say?"

"He got snotty with me. Told me I'd be happy to hear the incident cost him a job in our school district."

"It did? What'd you say?"

"I told him I wasn't happy, I was *over the moon!*"

The way she says it makes me laugh out loud. I am so relieved.

"Oh, Mom. That's the best. You're the best."

"I'm happy to hear you laughing. I've been afraid to tell you. I thought you'd be angry with me."

Angry? I might have been after it all went down, but now?

"Thanks for telling me, Mom. Your timing is perfect."

We talk for a long time after that. I tell her about the conversation with Mrs. Sullivan and about what Ricky said about my natural talent for music producing. I tell her about Reggie and the college tours, and when I ask her if I can keep living at the Jersey shore in the fall, she says okay.

"I'll miss you, honey. But you're in good hands, and you're only an hour away."

The conversation is going so well that I fear telling her the next bit of information.

"I want you to know, Mom. I'm working hard on my life plan, I really am. But there's still a possibility that Malcolm will be part of it. I know you said you didn't want me to go on tour in the fall. But…I might be going on tour in the fall."

There are a few moments of uncomfortable silence.

"I can't wait to hear your song. Mrs. Sullivan couldn't stop raving about it." Mom seems to ignore what I've said, making me wonder if she heard me. I'm about to repeat myself when she continues. "I wish I'd known how you felt about Lynn's accident sooner, baby. I could have helped you. I feel like you and I have wasted so much time. I love you more than anything. You know that, right? Things will be better."

My mother's voice is uncharacteristically tender and without its usual matter-of-factness. It fills me with a certainty I've either never known or must have forgotten. After all, Mom's was the first voice I'd ever heard. Intuitively, I trusted its timbre before I could speak, and I trust it now. She heard me just fine. This is her way of saying that whatever I decide, it's going to be all right.

It's the second best thing to happen to me today.

THIRTY-EIGHT

"Quinny!" Kiki startles me as I'm stocking shelves, and I wind up tossing two fistfuls of Smarties into the air like confetti.

I turn to find her standing in the candy aisle of the Ben Franklin with Liam's sister, Lucy. We've never officially met, but I've seen her at Keegan's with her boyfriend, Connor.

"Quinny, you know Lucy, right?"

I nod and smile as I bend to pick up the scattered Smarties. Lucy and Kiki crouch down to help.

"So you're the good twin?" I say. "He talks about you all the time. Almost as much as he talks about Andrew."

Lucy laughs. "I don't think he talks about anyone as much as he talks about Andrew."

Kiki frowns. "Hey!"

"I mean except for you, Keeks," Lucy wisely clarifies.

"He must be a great guy."

"He is. He's a best friend to both of us."

When we stand up, I get a better look at her. I know girl/boy twins can never be identical, but Lucy and Liam look nothing alike. He's dark-haired and light-eyed. She's the exact opposite. Side by side, they'd be a human yin-yang symbol.

"What are you doing Saturday night?" Kiki asks.

Waiting for Malcolm to call, I want to say. That's what I do every night. Even after all that's happened, I'm desperate to see him. I want to know where he and I stand, to hear that he's going to be all right and tell him that I will be too. I want to tell him I talked to Lynn's mom. It kills me that I haven't told him about the phone call yet. So much of what's happened is because of him. He's changed me. We've changed each other. Our paths collided and we propelled each other in the right direction. I'm willing to accept that it might not be the same direction, but I need to hear it from him.

"Nothing. I'm doing nothing."

Kiki squawks like a buzzer. "Wrong! It's girls' night out, and you're coming with us."

"I am?"

"Yes, you are! It's Lucy's last weekend home, and we're sending her off to Princeton with a bang."

Lucy shakes her head. "I keep telling Kiki, there will be no bang."

Kiki rolls her eyes playfully. "Lucy is 150 percent straight-edge. Prepare yourself for a night of G-rated entertainment."

I point at Kiki. "G-rated is fine with me. I could use a few more Bambi moments in my life." I'm actually excited. Aside from my sister, no one's ever invited me to a girls' night before. This almost makes up for not getting asked to prom.

"We'll pick you up at four thirty," Kiki says.

Four thirty? It seems a tad early for a girls' night out, but what the hell do I know? This is all new to me.

"See you then."

They arrive at my house late in the afternoon on Saturday, and from there, we walk to the Crab's Claw Inn for dinner. For the past two days, it's been nice having this diversion to look forward to. This is my seventh day of not seeing or talking to Malcolm, and I'm beginning to wonder if I ever will again.

Because it's so early, we pass lots of moms returning from the beach with Wonder Wheelers and small kids in tow, while bigger kids and adults head toward the ocean with surfboards and boogie boards. The waves must be good today.

The Crab's Claw Inn looks like the quintessential shore house, big and white with black shutters and a large wooden porch out front. Inside, there are two separate bars and seating areas: one downstairs where the living room and kitchen used to be, and one upstairs, where the bedrooms once were.

"Since we're here before five, dessert's *included*," Lucy says when the waitress is done taking our drink orders. "The early bird special also comes with soup or salad."

Ah. The four-thirty start time makes more sense now.

"Awesome!" I say. Lucy's geekdom is adorable, and I want to support her enthusiasm for free soup and dessert, even if we are dining with mostly senior citizens.

"Easy now," Kiki teases. "We've got a long night ahead of us. Pace yourselves."

I look at her over the menu. "You can pace yourself if you want. I plan on getting whipped cream *and* a cherry on top of my ice cream."

"And the lobster bisque," Lucy says. "You've got to try the lobster bisque."

After dinner, we walk back to Kiki's car and head to our next stop on Lucy's party train—Creativity Uncorked. It's one of those picture painting places, where middle-aged women get drunk on wine and paint sloppy acrylic landscapes to hang on their walls.

"We're doing seascapes tonight," Lucy says as we settle in behind our easels. "I thought it would be nice to have when I'm landlocked at Princeton. I can hang the painting in my dorm room."

Kiki opens the small cooler bag she brought in from the car and hands us each an orange mango iced tea. We place our bottles in the easel slots where the other women in the class are keeping their Pinots and Cabernets.

"You might want to hang *my* painting in your dorm room," Kiki says. "We all know I'm the artsy one."

Lucy looks at me. "She's right. I can't even draw an earthworm. The sketches I did for my bio labs looked like the work of a first grader."

"Yeah, but her lab notes are better than Marie Curie's," Kiki says.

Even though I don't say much as we paint, it's amusing to listen to the comfortable banter between two old friends as they work. They talk in shorthand, completing each other's sentences while reminiscing. I can't remember if Lynn and I were ever that way. For the past three years, keeping my anxiety at bay has meant suppressing all memories, good and bad. Even now, I'm reluctant to go there. Not when I'm having the nicest, most normal night I've had in, well, ever.

We're painting sunrises over the ocean, but I decide to go rogue and make mine over the bay, more specifically, the view from Malcolm's back deck. If it turns out okay, maybe I'll give it to him.

Because nothing says *Sorry we couldn't be friends* like an amateur seascape.

Kiki leans closer to her canvas and carefully dabs white

paint on the waves to create whitecaps that look like they're rolling. She's got skills.

"So, apparently my boyfriend is going on tour this fall," she says.

I let out an involuntary gasp. "Keeks, no! Liam decided to go?"

She nods. "I won't say this to him, but it's a total nightmare. I have to trust him. I *do* trust him. But thinking about him playing all those bars, in front of all those girls, while I'm here practicing dying hair and waxing eyebrows? It's going to be hard."

I turn to Lucy. "Your parents are okay with it?"

"He told them he'll defer his Rutgers' acceptance for a semester and start college this spring. Surprisingly, they agreed. I think they recognize he has talent and want to give him room to pursue his dream."

Kiki pouts as she rinses her brush. "Why couldn't they have done me a solid and forbade it? No pressure, Quinny, but I'd feel a whole lot better if I knew you were going too."

"Are you considering it?" Lucy asks.

"I was. But it may no longer be an option."

"You mean because they're auditioning drummers? *Pfft.* Liam says Malcolm wants to have a backup plan," Kiki says.

"I can understand that." After all, I *did* tell Malcolm to find another drummer. "Why hasn't Malcolm told me any of this? I haven't heard from him since our fight last weekend."

Kiki winces. "I think he's afraid to talk to you."

"You think or you know?" I ask.

"When I told him you needed time alone, he looked crushed. I wanted to hug the sadness right out of him. Plus, you did kind of quit the band."

She's right. He offered an olive branch, and I shut him down. "I messed up. So much was going on that night and I didn't handle it the way I should have."

"We've all been there. Text him. Make him think of you while he's auditioning those yahoos," Kiki says.

"What should I say?"

"How about 'hi' with an emoji," Keeks suggests.

"We've had zero contact in seven days and I should hit him with an emoji?"

Lucy jumps in. "From a communication standpoint, guys are far less complex than us. They don't need as many words."

"Listen to her—she's smart. Don't even say 'hi.' One good emoji is enough," Keeks says.

"Which one?" I ask.

"Quinny, Quinny, Quinny. You have much to learn. The cat wearing glasses, of course."

"There's a cat wearing glasses?"

Kiki holds out her hand. "Gimme your phone."

Once the emoji is located, I do what she says—and get an immediate reply.

"Well? What'd he say?" Kiki asks when she hears the *ping*.

I read my phone. "Call you later." My heart thuds in my chest.

"My work here is done," she says.

I think about my connection with Malcolm. He's the one person I've felt comfortable with telling my secrets to. I've missed having moments like this one. It feels good to have girlfriends again.

THIRTY-NINE

Malcolm doesn't call—he shows up. I should have expected it. It's kind of his thing.

Keeks pulls in Auntsie's driveway after our night of good, clean fun. I can't believe it's only 9:00 p.m. Malcolm is parked outside Auntsie's house in a gray van I don't recognize.

"Well, well, well. Look who the cat emoji dragged in. And you doubted its power," Keeks says.

"I never will again," I say.

Lucy exits the car to let me out of the back seat. Kiki exits the car to be nosey. She shades her eyes from the streetlight, where moths flutter in the yellow glow, and peers toward Malcolm's new ride. Guess he's getting ready for the tour.

"He looks different. Don't you think he looks different? And what's he doing sitting in that van like that?"

"Waiting for Quinn?" Lucy offers.

"Listen, Princeton, I don't need you to point out the obvious. I'm simply wondering if Quinn's aunt wouldn't let him in the house. He looks like a stalker."

I hadn't thought of that, but now I'm wondering the same thing. Did Auntsie kick him to the curb?

I open my arms to give Keeks a hug. "Thanks for inviting me to girls' night."

"You're welcome, Quinny. Next time, we'll road trip to Princeton and mingle with the smarties," Keeks jokes.

Lucy hugs me next. "Yes! Please visit!"

"Good luck at college," I say, though something tells me she's not the type who needs it.

Lucy whispers in my ear. "Good luck with Malcolm, but remember to do what's right for you."

"Thanks, I will." My voice cracks a little. Why am I choking up? I've known Lucy for about ten seconds. I guess I'm sensing the beginning of all the upcoming endings, and I don't like it. Or maybe it's bittersweet knowing that if things had turned out differently, I'd also be sending my best friend off to Princeton.

My chest tightens as I watch them drive away. If I skip the gig next weekend, who knows when I'll see them again? I meander down the crushed seashell driveway, still holding my painting, and into the street where Malcolm is parked. The driver's door window is open.

When I poke my head in to say "Hey," I get a good look at him. Keeks was right. He does look different.

"You shaved your beard!"

He runs a hand along his smooth chin.

"Yeah, I decided if I'm serious about becoming the guy I used to be, I should start by looking like him."

"What did that guy have that you don't?"

"A clean conscience, control, presence of mind, a band, a future...hubris and giant ego too, so I guess he wasn't perfect."

"Maybe the happy medium lies in a goatee or soul patch."

Malcolm bursts out laughing, and my shoulders relax.

"I missed you, Cat's Eye."

"Missed you too."

"Wanna go for ride? I've got a lot to tell you."

I nod. "Let me check in with my aunt."

I jog back up the driveway and open the screen door. Auntsie and Reggie are watching TV on the couch.

"For the record, I told him he was welcome to join me and Reg here while he waited," she says.

"That's a relief. I thought maybe he was denied entry."

"His choice. I told him he looked like a creeper in that van."

I laugh. "Kiki said the same thing. I'll be home by midnight."

"Okay, but *call* if that changes. None of this *I forgot to text* or *I'm having an impromptu pajama party*."

Her firm tone makes Reggie yip.

"Okay, okay. I will."

When I return to his truck and slip into the passenger side, I'm still holding my canvas.

"What's that?" Malcolm asks.

I hold it up. "A bad painting of one of my favorite views."

Malcolm studies it seriously, no mocking in his expression. "What are you going to do with it?"

"Weird that you should ask. I planned on giving it to you. That is, if I saw you again, which I am now, so here."

I hand it to him and he gently rests it on the bench seat behind us.

"Trade ya. It's the same view," he says and hands me an album. At first I think it's another vintage vinyl purchase for my aunt, but then my eyes finally comprehend what I'm seeing. My glasses are on the cover! They're perched on the dock at Malcolm's borrowed house, backed by the bay waters and a sunrise sky. The lenses reflect the images of Malcolm's guitar and my drumsticks. "Malcolm Trent" is scrawled across the top of the album cover in his handwriting and the title, *Cat's Eye*, is underneath.

"When did you do this?"

"I took the picture one morning before you woke up. A graphic artist has been helping me with the rest."

"You've been busy since I last saw you."

"Yep. It helped having something to do."

I turn the album over in my hands. The bay scene continues onto the back cover with the song titles written in Malcolm's hand across the waves.

"Hmph. So that's what the other songs are called!"

I run my fingers down the column of titles and see a sixth song has been added.

"Cat's Eye?"

"I needed a title track."

"Can I hear?"

"Wait until you're alone. Play it on your aunt's stereo."

"Should I ask what it's about?"

"To be honest, it started off as a song about addiction and wound up being about a girl."

"Anyone I know?" I ask.

Malcolm just smiles. I open the slit along the side of the album and pull out the paper sleeve that holds and protects the record. One side is covered with writing.

"You're listed as the cowriter for 'That Last Night,' and I may have said some nice stuff about you in the liner notes."

Liner notes are like the acknowledgments in a book, the artist's chance to thank people. Malcolm mentions everyone involved in the six-song project—even Auntsie gets a nod for feeding us. He includes a dedication to his two bandmates who died in the accident, and the last line is about me.

And finally, to Quinn, the real "Cat's Eye." Thank you for making everything better.

"What do you think?" Malcolm asks.

"It's beautiful."

"I was inspired." His smile and clean-shaven face make him look so much younger than the last time I saw him. It raises my hopes about the two of us getting a fresh start.

"Want to hear the rest of the songs?"

I nod.

He punches them up on his phone and then puts the van in drive.

I turn around and look into the back of the van. It's cavernous compared to a normal SUV.

"So, I guess you're getting ready for the road."

"It's been hectic, but in a good way. I traded in my pickup for this. It's not fancy, but it's only three years old and most importantly, it's safe. I had a few dates fall through and had to find other clubs to replace those gigs, but I made it happen. Plus, I've been getting the songs mastered in time to get CDs and albums pressed."

I wish we had talked about these decisions, but maybe I was never meant to be part of them.

The music plays as we drive along the coast to some unknown destination, or perhaps no destination at all, I don't know. He doesn't say and I don't ask; I'm simply relieved to have this time alone with him. I reach over and place my hand on his, which rests on his thigh. He hesitates, then flips his palm upward and intertwines his fingers with mine. Friends can hold hands, right?

When the music ends, I tell him the final mix sounds amazing.

He smiles big. "My old label thought so too. They're definitely sending an A&R person to the gig."

"Malcolm, that's fantastic! Why didn't you tell me?"

"I only found out yesterday. You were the first person I wanted to call."

"Why didn't you?"

"Because I was afraid. You said you wanted to be alone, and I'd already screwed up. I needed to get my life more in order before I saw you again. It killed me not to share the news with you immediately."

I squeeze his hand tighter. "Lynn's mom called me."

"What? When?" he said, shocked.

"Two days ago. It still seems so surreal."

I tell him the whole story about the letter and the cemetery and playing the song again. I fill him in about Ricky and my ideas about community college and studying audio engineering.

My words tumble out like I'm afraid that after this ride is over, so are we, and I'll never get the chance to share these things with him again.

"Oh, and I got real drums!"

"Your aunt showed me. Nice."

"Yeah, Sam Ash had to order them. They arrived this morning."

"You sound excited, Cat's Eye. I'm happy for you."

When we approach the inland waterway leading out to the ocean, Malcolm pulls into the parking lot and finds a spot. We stand by the rocks, watching the fishing boats go out for the night. I can tell something's on his mind.

"What is it?" I ask. "You can tell me."

He turns toward me and I expect him to hug me or at least hold my hand. I'm hoping this is all leading toward him saying we belong together. Instead, he folds his arms across his chest and tucks his hands against his elbows. It's like he put himself in a straitjacket.

I move toward him and he takes a step back. I'm trying hard not to be insulted.

"I don't bite. Not anymore anyway." My attempt to lighten the heaviness between us and stave off whatever's coming next fails.

"There's something I need to explain," he says.

"Okay."

"The whole time we were in the studio, I was feeling too much."

I scrunch my brow. "For me?"

"For everything. I'm out of practice with sitting with all that intense emotion, and my first instinct was to run from it. I needed a mental break from the memories of friends I've lost, the logistics of this new project and tour…us. I needed to be by myself for a while to deal with all of that. But we were on a strict deadline with Ricky and I couldn't. I felt trapped, and because of that, I stumbled…"

"It was one Vicodin though, right?"

"Yes. I haven't used since, but I felt like shit afterward. I never should have taken that beer from Travis. It loosened my resolve. I'm not as strong as I thought I was, and I'm ashamed of how I acted."

"Don't be. I'm sorry about what happened that night. I was too hard on you. I got scared too."

He unfolds his arms and closes the space between us. "Quinn, wait. Hear me out. Since then, I've been going to two meetings a day and have been in constant contact with my sponsor. The urges I'm having to use scare me. And one pill, one beer is too much for me. I *cannot* afford to slide."

"Maybe the tour should wait. Why does it have to happen now? See what the A&R person says. They might sign you and pay for a tour. That would give you more time."

It will give us more time, I want to say, but know better than to scare him a second time. He doesn't need the pressure of "us" with everything else.

Malcolm shakes his head. "On the road I'll be busy, I'll have a purpose. This tour has always been about something bigger than me. I owe it to those guys. It's part of me making amends. It's my penance."

I get that. I *so* get that. "What about meetings?"

"I'll go as often as I can. I've already looked up the NA chapters between here and Florida, and I'll check in with my sponsor every day."

"Have you thought this through?"

"I have. Plus, all signs point to this being the right time to tour. Travis is available, my parents sold the house, Liam's signed on."

I knew about Travis and Liam, but the news about the house brings an unexpected lump to my throat. Even though it wasn't ours, for a little while at least, it felt like home.

I'm afraid to ask.

"What about a drummer?"

He lets out a long sigh.

"I offered the spot to a guy we auditioned today. He's a total pro, and he digs the songs." Malcolm reaches out and touches my fingertips. "But I made it very clear to him, to everyone, if you're in, we'll find a spot for you. Maybe you can play percussion or do sound?"

So now I'm Tambourine Girl?

"What about the gig next weekend?" I ask.

"That's up to you."

He gets points for not wanting to hurt my feelings, but he's not exactly telling me he wants me beside him or professing his undying love, is he?

"It's probably best if the new guy plays the showcase. You've got a lot riding on it, and you guys need to gel before you hit the road." My voice cracks, betraying how hard this is for me.

"Are you sure, Cat's Eye? This is your record too. You should at least play on a couple of songs."

Is he disappointed? I can't tell. Anyway, it's hard to feel sorry for him because, newsflash, I'm holding on by a few gossamer-thin threads here.

"I'm sure. Anyway, with Liam playing guitar, someone will have to do sound at Keegan's. I'll let Caleb know I can work."

Caleb can handle the soundboard better than I can, but I'm trying to make lemonade here.

"Well, if you change your mind, about any of it, let me know. We're friends—I want you there."

I want to be there. For all of it. I want to be at each one of those twenty-three gigs from here to Gainesville, making sure he stays on track and doesn't slide on the road. I want to see this tour through the end. I couldn't bear it if anything bad happened to him. So why don't I say all that? Why am I holding back? Probably because he's making me feel like how Reggie must have felt every time I got his hopes up during a walk and then returned him to his cage. I'm sorry for hurting that sweet, furry guy with my lack of commitment.

"Okay. If I change my mind, I'll let you know."

Malcolm reaches for my glasses, but instead of pushing them up like he usually does, he takes them off and looks at me. Then he cups my cheek with one hand and traces my chin with his thumb. My cheeks flush with a mixture of anger and excitement. I think he's going to kiss me, but he takes my hand and pulls me into a hug. I resist at first, but soon give in. I've missed the weight of his arms around me. I rest my head on his shoulder and press my lips against his neck.

"Friends are allowed to do this?" I whisper.

"We'll make sure our new contract includes a clause."

I pull away and take back my glasses.

I don't want a new contract.

I don't want the old contract.

I want him to tell me to never let go.

FORTY

Auntsie's still awake when Malcolm drops me off. Reggie, however, is passed out cold. I'm beginning to realize the secret life of dogs is not so secret after all. They sleep, a lot. But when they're awake, they treat people the way people should treat people—with unabashed love and devotion.

"Whatcha got?" Auntsie nods toward the album.

I hold it up and show her the picture.

"Should I pack your bags?" she asks when she recognizes my glasses and sees the album title.

My lips curl into a half-hearted smile. Which is exactly how my conversation with Malcolm has made me feel.

"He wrote a song called 'Cat's Eye.'"

She slaps her knees and stands up.

"I'm gonna get started. You'll send me postcards from the road, right?"

I hate to squash her enthusiasm. "Not so fast. I haven't heard the song yet."

She puts out her hand. "Give it here. The curiosity is killing me."

"It's the last track."

She cues up the record and we both stand, watching it turn like it's a YouTube video and there'll be something to see.

It's a simple song, a beautiful song, with Malcolm singing and playing alone on acoustic guitar. I like it this way, without a band. It's easier to imagine he's talking to me. He sings about longing and desire, love that makes the pain goes away, a euphoria that never lasts. He uses the pronoun *she*, but I recognize the lyrics' ambiguity. This could easily be a song about drugs, and I wonder if maybe it is after all, except that it's called "Cat's Eye."

When the song's over, she tries to hide it, but I can see Auntsie has tears in her eyes. But me? I'm too filled with doubt. Auntsie keeps her head down and pretends to read the lyrics and liner notes.

"I'm so glad he took the time to make vinyl copies. Downloading a three-minute single to your phone *is* convenient, but one song doesn't tell the whole story. It's like reading a chapter instead of the entire book," she says.

She's right. She's holding our whole story, except I don't know how it ends.

"Goodnight, Auntsie," I say. "You can keep that copy for your shelf."

Upstairs, I text Malcolm before I fall asleep.

Loved the song

I hoped you would

Thank you

Any time, Cat's Eye

More like *out of time*, not anytime, because that's what we are. Unless I decide to be his groupie this fall. The more I think about it, when he dropped me off, after a night of him laying out the very specific parameters for how I can be part of his life, he never mentioned wanting to see me this week. *Sounds like Malcolm is taking care of Malcolm*, I hear my aunt say. Yeah, well. I've got parameters too.

See you at the Keegan's gig

Not before?

Can't. Sorry. Mom and sister here all week

You can come over and watch movies

"Friends" probably shouldn't do that

I'll leave the door open if you change your mind.

Thx. I won't

That's a lie. I will. But I won't act on it. Not anymore. It's time I start putting myself first.

On Monday evening, I'm walking home from my shift at the Ben Franklin, my melancholy amplified by the hint of fall in the bay breeze, when my phone rings. It's a Nashville cell phone number I don't recognize. I figure it's a telemarketer and almost hit Ignore, but I answer it.

"Hey, girl!" Ricky croons when I pick up.

It's only been a little more than a week since we recorded together, but oh, how I've missed that Southern charm.

"Ricky! I've been meaning to call you, but I didn't want to bother you."

"Never a bother, Quinn Gallo. Never a bother. You got a sec?"

"Sure."

"I wanna run something by you."

I figure he wants to talk about Malcolm, or his music, or both. But what he says leaves me feeling like it's the universe, not Ricky Keyes, who's calling and maybe, just maybe, we're finally square.

I hang up and round the corner with an uncontrollable smile on my face as Mom's minivan, Old Bessie, pulls into the driveway. We've logged a lot of memories and miles in Old Bessie, and it's a comfort to see she's still running.

"Mom!" I wave to her from up the block as she gets out of the van. She's already in beach mode with a brown spaghetti strap sundress and flip-flops. Evie, Ashley, and Kate pile out of the passenger side. For some reason I can't fully explain, I start running and don't stop until Mom and I are hugging. I nearly knock her over with my beagle-like enthusiasm. I breathe in her familiar perfume, and think about how badly I missed this when we were keeping each other at arm's length. It makes me sad to think that the last time we hugged like this, I was shorter than her.

"Let me help you load in," I say, using band-speak.

She clicks her key fob and opens the hatch. The van is packed top to bottom with suitcases, beach chairs, boogie boards, a Wonder Wheeler, an umbrella, and bags and bags of groceries.

"Holy shit! Are we preparing for the apocalypse?"

Evie hefts her duffel bag over her shoulder. "You know Mom. She always buys way too much food."

Auntsie reaches into the van and grabs four ShopRite bags, two in each hand.

"Don't knock it. This annual visit keeps me stocked with food until Columbus Day."

"Let us help with that," Ashley says, coming to the back of the van with Kate.

When the trunk is unloaded, there's barely an inch of hardwood floor left uncovered. My drums make the living room feel extra tight. Reggie runs around, peeking into each grocery bag and sniffing everyone's luggage. When Mom pulls out a brand-new squeaky toy for him, he nearly hyperventilates.

"Girls, why don't you take your bags upstairs? Gemma, your room's all ready for you. Quinn cleared her stuff out yesterday," Auntsie says to Mom.

"Don't be silly. I can stay here on the couch. It's Quinn's room now." Mom smiles at me.

Who is this woman?

"Mom, it's okay. This is your vacation."

"I insist." She plops herself on the couch, and Reggie takes the opportunity to launch himself onto the cushion beside her with his stuffed chipmunk, and then resumes his attempts to extract the source of its squeak. "This is very comfortable. Plus, I'm an early riser. I don't want to wake you girls when I go out for my walks or make coffee."

"Are you sure? Your quarters come with a dog, you know," I tell Mom. "He didn't take to his crate or our beds the way we thought he would. He's claimed the couch as his domain."

Mom laughs and puts her hand on Reggie's back. He drops his toy and jumps up to kiss her face. Grateful guy.

"I don't mind sharing if he doesn't. He won't take up much space."

"No, but he snores," Auntsie says.

"What time do you take your walks?" I ask Mom.

"Around sunrise, why?"

"Okay if I go with you one morning?"

"You can go with me every morning."

For the next few days, I feel like I'm vacationing at the Jersey shore. I'm out walking on the boardwalk every morning with Mom and logging more beach time and eating more funnel cake than I have all summer.

Evie, Ashley, and Kate like to head up to the beach early every day to stake out a good spot near the water, then promptly fall back to sleep in the sun. When I'm not at the Ben Franklin, I join them and sit under the umbrella with a book. I'm way behind on Auntsie's reading list, and Virginia Woolf is proving to be more challenging than I expected. I love the stream-of-consciousness style, but it's not exactly beach read material. Plus, it's taking for freaking ever for the Ramsay family to get to that damn Scottish lighthouse already. By Friday, I abandon the Woolf novel and decide to go to a lighthouse myself.

"*Where?*" Evie asks through a mouthful of pancakes. She heard me. I can tell she's not into it.

"To a lighthouse. I think we should go visit a lighthouse," I say.

"Uh, why?" Kate's about as enthusiastic as Evie, but tries to be nice.

"Because I have the whole day off, and I don't want to spend it sitting on the beach."

Ashley gasps at my Jersey shore blasphemy.

Mom takes a sip of her coffee.

"Which lighthouse did you want to visit, hon?"

"I'm not sure."

Auntsie perks up. "Well, Sandy Hook Lighthouse is the oldest working lighthouse in the country. Absecon is the tallest in New Jersey, Cape May is the farthest, and 'Old Barney,' that's Barnegat Lighthouse, is the closest."

"And you know all that because?" Evie asks.

"Uh, coastal town librarian?" I can hear the *duh* in her voice.

"How about we visit Cape May?" Mom says. "I haven't been there since we were girls."

"Okay if we stay here?" Evie asks.

"Fine. But swim between the lifeguard flags."

The girls giggle.

"We don't swim, Mrs. Gallo. We stare at our phones and tan," Kate explains.

"Even better. I won't worry as much," Mom says.

"Well, I have to work, but you two enjoy yourselves," Auntsie says. "Wear comfortable shoes. It's 217 steps to the top." Auntsie shakes her head as she shuffles toward her bedroom. "And I wonder why all the kids come to me when they're writing reports. I've got to get myself a life."

FORTY-ONE

When your fitness routine consists of exactly one sit up a day—the one you do each morning when you get out of bed—walking up 217 steps on a never-ending cast iron spiral staircase is tough. Every so often, we have to pull over to let people descending pass, and I, for one, welcome the break.

"Is it possible to get altitude sickness in a lighthouse? Did the sign say anything about it?"

Mom laughs. "This is a lighthouse, not Denver."

Mom made a joke. Interesting.

We wait for a young couple with three little kids to go by before resuming our climb.

"So," Mom says. She's walking in front of me, huffing and

puffing and holding the stitch in her side. "How's the application to community college coming?"

"Almost finished. There's not much too it. I still have plenty of time to register for October classes." I'm breathing as heavy as she is and using the rail to pull myself along as we climb.

"Still thinking about a writing course and psychology?" she asks over her shoulder.

"Maybe music theory too."

Mom nods. "Good. They sound like the kind of credits that would transfer."

In addition to playing the part of the tourist this week, I've been taking some time to get my shit together. I'm not going to lie, I was secretly hoping for some change of heart from Malcolm—an excuse to abandon my online application. Something more than: "You can follow me to Florida and play tambourine if you want to." But that didn't happen, and what he's offering isn't enough. I can't keep waiting.

"And the band? You're okay with your decision?"

"Yeah. I told Malcolm I haven't changed my mind."

We're almost to the top. A middle-aged couple in matching polo shirts and visors are descending, and Mom and I have to squish ourselves against the wall to let them by. I wait until they're gone to start talking.

"I'll still be at the gig tomorrow night. I wouldn't miss it." It is, after all, the record release party for an album I helped create.

"An A&R person from Malcolm's old label is going to be there. Malcolm hired a professional drummer for the tour. That's who should be playing the showcase and the tour, not me."

Maybe I'd feel differently if I were Malcolm's girlfriend. But I'm not.

We finally reach the top and emerge through the door out onto the enclosed platform. The colors seem so bright after the darkness in the stairwell. The view is spectacular, and the waves sound like hushed voices below.

"This view is better than from the free fall tower." I can take my time and look as long as I want. I like being more in control of gravity.

"The sign says we're one hundred and sixty-five feet above sea level," Mom says.

We circle the tower, taking in the views from all sides— Cape May Harbor and Wildwood Crest to the north, Delaware Bay to the west, and to the east, nothing but the vast Atlantic Ocean. A small motorboat, like a shooting star, slices a white path through water the color of Medusa's curls. I turn my face toward the sun, close my eyes, and breathe in the fresh salty air. My heart slows, and I'm hit with an unfamiliar calm. I am 217 steps away from the life waiting for me below, and I want to forget about it for a while. My thoughts reach past this summer, the scandalous conclusion to my lackluster high school career, the accident, all my bad choices…

"Remember how Lynn and I used to build fairy houses and leave them all over the yard?"

Mom smiles. "I do."

I open my eyes and stare straight ahead, looking but not seeing. "We used shoe boxes and baskets and ribbons and whatever else we could find in the craft drawer."

"Once you used an entire jar of glitter glue."

"You weren't happy about that."

"It's still embedded in our kitchen floor."

"No it's not," I protest.

"It is. Glitter is evil. Keep that in mind when you have kids someday."

"Lynn had this book with black-and-white photos of fairies taken by these two cousins like a hundred years ago. Supposedly they were real."

"The Cottingley Fairies. It was a hoax, but you two were convinced fairies were real."

I laugh. "And yet we doubted their ability to conjure suitable housing."

I press my hands against the safety fence. Mom's eyes glance at the cuff bracelet on my wrist.

"I didn't want to die, you know," I say quietly.

And it's true. I had started off scratching and cutting myself in places no one could see. My upper thigh, my lower belly. That day, I don't know what possessed me to cut my wrist, but I knew as soon as I pierced that thin skin above my bluish veins that I'd gone too far. I was terrified.

Mom puts her hand on mine. "That was the single worst day of my life."

I unsnap the leather bracelet. The skin underneath is a blinding beacon of white. It's been years since it's seen the sun. I turn my wrist up and trace my scar.

"I've been thinking about getting a tattoo to cover it. Something with Lynn's initials, maybe. Auntsie knows an artist who does good work." I shrug. "Who knows? Guess I'll wait and see. In the meantime, I don't think I want to wear this anymore."

"What are you going to do with it?"

"Would it be weird if I left it here?"

She pulls me into a side hug. "Come on. I'll help you find a hiding spot."

FORTY-TWO

The next day, I work a double shift at the Ben Franklin, hoping to keep my mind off the fact that I would otherwise be getting ready for my one and only gig with my short-lived band. Instead, I can think of nothing else while I'm in the throes of the end-of-summer blowout at the five-and-ten.

We have tons of stuff on sale. Mugs, T-shirts, car magnets, key chains—everyone is snatching up their tiny piece of the Jersey shore to display in cubicles and on kitchen counters and refrigerators until next summer. I work through my lunch and dinner breaks and wind up eating an entire bag of Twizzlers in my car as I ride over the bridge to my second job. I volunteered to work because, while I wanted to be there to show my support, it's not going to be easy to be a voyeur to what could have been.

Keeping busy will make it easier to not be seated behind the drum kit. Maybe.

By the time I get to Keegan's, the opening band is already on and the room is buzzing. Last night at work, Liam told me he and Malcolm had been posting about tonight's gig on social media to get the word out.

"With the label guy coming, Malcolm wanted to make sure we weren't playing to an empty venue," he said.

Whatever they did, it worked.

My eyes pan the room looking for Liam, Kiki, Arnie, or anyone else I know. My breath catches when I see Malcolm. He's standing at the far side of the "stage," bookended by Trent and Liam and looking all clean-shaven and rocker-like in a tight black shirt and ripped jeans. He's talking to a woman I don't recognize, but she's sporting her best New York hipster attire, so I assume she's from the label. She keeps touching Malcolm's arm when she talks to him, stoking my jealousy and longing. I try to shrug it off as I duck behind the bar and grab my apron. I have no idea how tonight is going to play out, but my pulse is already racing.

"Hey, Quinn," Caleb says as he fills a mug at the tap. "Can you do me a favor and adjust the bass on the board? It's too loud."

"Sure."

I notice he's looking spiffier than usual with an actual button-down shirt, black jeans, and boots as opposed to his usual

T-shirt, cargo shorts, and Converse high-tops. Caleb looks like an adult.

"And when you're finished, can you help with barbacking now that Liam is a rock star?"

I guess he kind of is, isn't he? I'm happy for Liam, but nervous for Kiki. I can't think of many girls who would be rooting for their boyfriends to go on the road without them. Too many temptations, although Liam's not the cheating type. Neither is Malcolm. With him, it's obviously the "drugs" part of "sex, drugs, and rock and roll" that I worry about. Though I have to remind myself that along with drumming duties, I've been relieved of my pseudo girlfriend role too.

I work my way through the crowd and make the required adjustments to the board as unobtrusively as possible. My eyes dart sideways, seeking out Malcolm like a divining rod drawn to water. He's still engaged in conversation with the woman from the label. Now they're leaning close, cupping each other's ear to be heard over the band. At one point, he looks up and sees me. He breaks into a grin, holds my gaze, and puts up his hand. Emotion tugs at my heart. I smile and wave back, hoping my face doesn't betray all I'm feeling. Suddenly, the ten feet between us seems more like a chasm.

I retreat to the bar and feel a hand on my elbow before I scoot around the other side.

"Q!"

"Liam! You're looking good, but you probably knew that."

He smirks, and I can tell he's proud of his charcoal gray

skinny jeans and the hint of product in his hair. Kiki's fine handiwork, no doubt.

He opens his arms and I hug him, letting a summer's worth of shared experiences pass between us. Who knew after this douchebag called me a Benny back in June we'd end up as friends?

We separate, and he puts his hands on my shoulders.

"Tell me you've changed your mind?"

I shake my head. "Kill it tonight, okay?"

"You belong up there with us."

I place a hand on the bar. "I belong right here. Somebody's got to be the barback now that you're about to become famous. Besides, you need to play this showcase with the new guy. Get one gig under your belt before you leave. I'm good."

I say I'm good but really, me being here tonight is how Malcolm described wanting drugs—like being on a diet surrounded by all my favorite foods. Or maybe it's more like standing on the platform watching my train leave. Either way, this night is not going to be easy for me, but I'll get through it. And then I'll get on with it.

"Quinny!" Kiki screeches my name as she emerges from the crowd behind Liam.

I lean down and kiss her cheek. "You look smoking tonight!"

She smiles and flips a thumb toward Liam. "Needed to remind him what he'll be missing."

"He won't forget. You should find yourself a spot up front. Is Lucy coming?"

"She's going to try. Princeton's already keeping her busy. Hopefully Connor and Andrew will represent."

"Ah, so I'll get to meet the one and only Andrew."

"I'll introduce you when he gets here."

I nod my head toward the bar behind me. "Caleb needs me."

She squeezes my hand. "Go."

I stand beside Caleb and immediately start washing glasses.

"So, I hear your aunt is making her musical debut tonight."

The soapy mug I'm holding nearly slips from my fingers. "What did you say?"

"Your aunt. She's living out her rock and roll dream and sitting in on cowbell."

No. Effing. Way.

As if on cue, Auntsie enters with her entourage—Mom, Evie, Kate, and Ashley.

Caleb chuckles. "It's funny, I always used to tease her about wanting to get in on my act."

"I had no idea they were coming."

Auntsie calls out and waves. "Quinn, babe!"

I force a smile and raise a wet hand. Dishwater trickles down my arm to my elbow. I'm wearing the vintage combat boots and sleeveless plaid shirt I had on the night I met Malcolm. I was hoping for closure through symmetry. Auntsie on cowbell throws that balance all out of whack.

"She didn't tell you?" Caleb looks both happy and amused

as Auntsie and company walk toward us. "She asked my advice about classic rock songs that were heavy on cowbell."

He pours two glasses of Pinot and has them ready by the time Auntsie and Mom reach the bar.

"Oh, and I think your sister is singing backup later on," he whispers from the corner of his mouth.

What the hell is going on here tonight?

"Ladies!" Caleb calls as they approach.

Auntsie beams, while Mom barely cracks a grin. Old grudges die hard, I guess. But Caleb doesn't seem to notice. He only has eyes for Auntsie as he leans over the bar to take their hands and kiss their cheeks.

"You missed sound check," Caleb jokes.

Auntsie holds up her bell and a drumstick. "This doesn't need a mic."

"Is that my drumstick?" I ask.

"Yep. Got the other one right here." She pats her bag, then lifts her wineglass and chinks Mom's. "Cheers!"

Mom looks at me. "I think your aunt's having a midlife crisis."

Auntsie swallows a big mouthful of white wine. "I beg to differ. I'm living the dream."

I turn to Evie, slightly hurt that she didn't tell me she'd be singing tonight. "What about you? Are you living the dream too?"

"Malcolm's hoping I can convince you to play on 'That Last Night.'"

He'd texted me earlier today trying to convince me to do the same.

Come on. It's only one song.

I don't want just one of anything.

I know it was unfair to throw his words back at him, and I wasn't trying to be insensitive and compare my feelings to an addiction, but I needed for him to understand how I feel. I thought he did. Apparently not. I look at Evie, who's waiting to hear what I have to say.

"I can't," I say. Then I walk down the bar to gather dirty glasses and fill the bowls with Chex Mix. I notice Arnie and Spoon Man on the end of the bar and say "Hi!" I sense my family talking about me as I move out of earshot, but I don't care.

"Hey, baby girl," Arnie slurs. "I'm feeling a tad under the weather, but I came out to hear you play."

I'm pretty sure it's not the "weather" Arnie's under.

I'm about to throw black coffee on his alcohol binge and tell him I'm not playing drums tonight, when he adds, "Who knows if I'll ever get another chance? We're all on a one-way trip, know what I'm saying, baby girl?"

Isn't there a saying about the wisdom of drunks? Or maybe it's babies. Either way, Arnie brings up a good point. The next time I show up for work, all of this will be over. Malcolm and

Liam will be in Maryland, Mom and Evie will be back in North Jersey, Auntsie will have retired her cowbell (I hope). Perhaps Arnie will have found himself another dive bar.

As right as Arnie may be, I'm still not playing this set. He'll be disappointed, but I'll make it up to him.

"Thanks, Arnie. Did you know you get a free appetizer with your Bud Light tonight?"

"I do? I've been coming here for years and I've never gotten a goddamn thing for free before."

"Well, tonight is your lucky night. What'll it be? Chicken fingers, nachos, wings?" Buying him an appetizer is the least I can do.

"I can't decide between nachos and calamari."

"How about both?" I point my chin toward Spoon Man. "You can share."

By the time I work my way back down the bar to put in Arnie's food order, the opening act has finished and Auntsie has left to join Malcolm and the band on stage. Five minutes later, they're set up and ready to go. Auntsie counts them in on the cowbell and Liam lays into this '70s-sounding guitar groove.

"Yeah! Blue Oyster Cult!" Caleb screams on his return from introducing the band. "This was my suggestion. No other rock song in history features this much cowbell."

He's not kidding. Auntsie is nonstop wailing on that thing in a somewhat ironic way, which is good because it's making Liam, Malcolm, and Trent smile and offering levity to a song titled "(Don't Fear) The Reaper." Probably wouldn't have been my first choice for a set opener, but the crowd seems into it.

"Wow, Liam is shredding that guitar solo," Caleb says.

"No kidding."

He's getting a chance to show off those superior skills he's always telling us about, and the new drummer is handling a part that would have had me barely hanging on. Add to that Malcolm's sweet vocals, Travis's harmonies, and Auntsie's enthusiasm, and they sound like a band. One that's been playing together much longer than a week.

Minus Auntsie, this is what Malcolm needed, not me. He's must be thinking the same thing. I'm relieved to be behind the bar, not up onstage holding him back.

When the song ends, Malcolm has Auntsie take a bow.

"Annie Gallo on cowbell, everyone."

Caleb claps his hands and gives a soul-piercing whistle through his teeth.

"Annie!" he screams and throws his arms up touchdown-style. My aunt, the rock star, catches his eye. She's beaming. Tonight probably won't be the start of her cowbell career, but it might be the reboot of a '90s love that lay dormant, waiting for the reaper to bring it back to life.

After Auntsie steps off the stage and reverts back to being

a music fan and librarian, Malcolm and the guys continue their set, playing four of the new songs in a row before mixing in some songs from the Gatsby years. I'm so busy I haven't had a chance to do more than hug Auntsie after her song before traipsing back to the bar to wash glasses, retrieve food orders, and restock the bar fridge with cold bottles of beer and fruity vodka and tequila drinks from the storage room.

Malcolm's oozing confidence and swagger tonight, his role as a front man fully restored since the first time I saw him play here. I'm happy for him, but at the same time, I can't wait for his set to be over so we can both get on with our separate lives.

I'm carrying a tray loaded with appetizers from the back to the bar when Malcolm and I lock eyes and I freeze. He's alone onstage with his acoustic guitar, while the band takes a break. He addresses the crowd but stares directly at me.

"We only have two more songs for you tonight. Both are from my new album, which is available for purchase tonight at the merch table." Malcolm pauses to point to Kiki, who waves to the crowd from behind the table that's laden with CDs, vinyl, stickers, and all things Malcolm Trent.

"You can also download these songs at all the usual places. Now that my shameless plug is over, I'm going to play the title track, 'Cat's Eye.' I once joked that this song started off being about drugs and ended up being about a girl. That was a lie. It's always been about a girl."

I forget that I'm standing in the middle of the crowd holding a tray until Auntsie swoops in to rescue the food, followed by Evie, Mom, and Kiki, who swoop in to rescue me. To say I've got all the feels right now would be an understatement. I'm embarrassed, touched, humbled, and grateful. Even if Malcolm and I have nothing else, we have this.

I'm surrounded by love and it's perfect.

When the song ends, half the room turns to look at me, but my eyes stay fixed on Malcolm. With a quick nod toward the drum kit, he beckons me toward the stage. I shake my head.

"Hey, everyone, guess what? As a special treat tonight, Quinn Gallo is going to sit in on drums for this last song."

I'm still shaking my head as Malcolm nods his. We're warming up for a standoff when Mom whispers in my ear.

"Can you do it for them, baby?"

I turn to see Lynn's parents waving from the bar. *Holy shit!* When did they get here? Mrs. Sullivan raises a glass and smiles, and *whoosh*, just like that, all the fight leaves me. Mom helps me take off my apron, then gently nudges me toward the stage. There's a smattering of applause as Auntsie hands me my sticks. My sister follows me and squeezes my hand before she moves to stand behind Travis's vocal mic. I get myself situated behind the drums and signal to Malcolm when I'm ready. He's standing behind his keyboard, which is angled to face me. This time, I want to see him as we play this song.

"This is 'That Last Night,'" he says, then begins to play those hauntingly beautiful opening chords.

We're minus a cellist and standup bass, but Travis does the song justice with his electric bass and my sister's backing vocals are plenty for this small room. Chills ripple up and down my arms. I breathe deep, filling my lungs and my heart with the energy of the room. I look into as many faces as possible as I await my part. I want to remember this.

Malcolm starts the third verse, and Liam steps toward me to exchange a knowing look that means *it's about time we join this party.* I tap the hi-hat and Liam strums his guitar, and I try not to think about how this is the last time we'll play together before they all leave and I go back to being Quinn Gallo, not Q, or Cat's Eye, or even Quinny.

I'm ready for whatever happens when the song ends. My heart's light and my body's in control as I let go of my anger, my fears, and my regrets and allow myself to experience the pure joy of making music with my friends.

Before I know it, the song's over. We turn to face one another, all smiles as the last notes fade from the keyboard and we hear the applause. Twice this song sent me running, but tonight I stay put, accepting that this is the last time I will be connected to these people in this particular way.

"Thank you, everyone. Good night," Malcolm says, and the room erupts with a swirl of activity. I'm hugging Evie, Kate,

Ashley, Liam, Kiki, Mom, the Sullivans. It's like a clown car emptying, with everyone I've ever known coming at me. I see Mom talking to Malcolm, and I want to go over, but I owe it to the Sullivans to stay here and talk to them.

"I can't believe you made the trip to see me," I say.

"We wouldn't have missed it, hon," Mrs. Sullivan says.

Mr. Sullivan smiles nervously, like he's afraid to say anything more. We stick to small talk after that, each of us sensing that it's the only safe ground. Once they leave, and the crowd finally settles down, I scan the room for Malcolm. He's stepping outside with the woman from the record label. He gives me a helpless shrug when he sees me, but I'm not jealous anymore. It's business, though I still wish we could have shared a moment before it was all over.

After I say my goodbyes and so longs to my family and friends, Caleb bellows from behind the bar.

"Quinn! Liam! If you two divas are done, I could use some help with cleanup." I glance toward the stage. Malcolm's gear is all packed up and stacked on the side, so I'm assuming he hasn't left for good yet.

"Hey, baby girl. That was outstanding," Arnie says.

I clear the empty plates from the appetizers that he and Spoon Man shared and wipe down the bar in front of him.

"Thanks, Arnie."

"I'm glad I got to hear you play." He stands to leave, and I notice there are tears in his bloodshot eyes.

"Don't worry, Arnie. Liam's leaving on tour, but I'll still be here."

"Good. This place would be just another shit hole without you."

He gives me a small salute, and then he's gone, along with everyone else it seems. Liam's nowhere to be found.

I get to work washing glasses and upending chairs onto tables so the cleaning crew can sweep and mop the floors.

"Why don't you take off, Quinn. I got this," Caleb says when he comes in from taking out the trash. "I think Malcolm's waiting outside for you."

"You sure you don't need me to stay?"

"Positive. I'm glad you're sticking around this fall. Arnie's right—this place would be a shit hole without you."

I smile. "Thanks, Caleb."

"See you tomorrow."

"Tomorrow?"

I don't usually work on Sundays. Not much happens at Keegan's then.

"Your aunt invited me over for a barbecue."

I give him a conspiratorial smile. "Bring dog biscuits and Pinot Grigio if you want to score extra points."

"Thanks, Quinn."

I take off my apron, and turn to leave when Caleb calls me back.

"Quinn?"

"Yeah?"

"Me and your aunt. I'm not sure how much she told you, but I'm the one who screwed up. Musicians, we're not... Let's say I spent my twenties trying to make my teens last as long as possible. I didn't deserve all she was willing to give."

I'm not sure if this is a confession or a warning.

"I don't think she sees it that way." Well, except for the arrested development part. She'd totally agree with that.

"That's because she's always been a better person than me. Anyway, I want you to know, if I get a second chance, it's because of you."

"I feel the same way about you and this place," I say. "I probably should have said this sooner, but thank you."

"You're welcome."

The exchange leaves us both a bit flustered and we talk over each other, me saying I'm going to take off as he simultaneously shoos me out the door with his dishrag. I'm relieved we didn't have to hug it out.

I push open the door to the parking lot and sense Malcolm before I see him. He's leaning against the building and snaps to attention when he sees me.

"Cat's Eye. I've been waiting for you."

I flick a thumb over my shoulder. "I was helping Caleb with the—"

He cuts me off with a gentle kiss on the lips. "I've been wanting to do that all night."

I step back. "I thought that was against the new rules."

"About that, Cat's Eye. I fucked up. What else is new, right?" He moves closer, reaching for my hand and playing with my fingertips. "I miss you. I miss playing music with you, the way you bite your lower lip when you play drums. I miss having you fall asleep next to me. I haven't slept more than three straight hours in two weeks. Nothing's been the same since that night at the studio. And I know it's my fault, so I only have myself to blame. I'm sorry. I'm so, so sorry."

"I'm sorry too. We were both wrong. That's what happens when friends fight."

He places his hands on my hips.

"I don't want us to be friends, Cat's Eye. That's what I'm trying to say. I don't want us to be apart. I know I have no right to ask you this, but come with me on this tour, please. I want you there, I need you there."

Why couldn't he have said this sooner? I'm annoyed and yet his words, his touch, the way all my senses come alive when we're standing this close, make me want to leave with him right now. But I can't be sure he won't change his mind tomorrow.

"You say these things, Malcolm, and then you take them back. You hinted that you loved me, but when I asked you who I was to you—"

"I made one of the biggest mistakes of my life, and that says a lot coming from an ex-junkie. I should have said *everything*. You are everything to me, Cat's Eye, and I don't want to let you go. I spent the past hour talking to some record label person who made me the types of promises I've been dying to hear, and all I could think about was getting back to you."

"Malcolm, I don't know. I finally had a life plan. A way to make my life work here, without you. You can't do this now. This isn't fair."

"I know, I know. You're right. Look, don't decide now. Promise me you'll think about it. Seriously think about it."

He leans in and kisses my forehead and each cheek before brushing his lips against mine. His eyes ask permission. I answer him by kissing him back, tentatively at first but in a way that dispels the notion that he and I could ever be only friends.

"I should go. My family's waiting up for me," I say when we separate.

Malcolm is still kissing my neck, sending shivers across my skin.

"Promise me you'll think about what I said?"

"Promise," I say. But I'm pretty sure my mind's already made up.

FORTY-THREE

It's the day before Labor Day, that last hurrah before the ceremonial end of summer. Newscasters love to remind us summer isn't *really* over until September twenty-something, but why kid ourselves? We know it's done. Mom and Evie will be leaving tomorrow morning. School starts on Tuesday, the same day Malcolm and the band leave. The big question is, will I be going with them? I hardly slept last night thinking about how I was going to bring this up with my family.

"I think I might be going on tour," I blurt out to Mom, Evie, and Auntsie, as we swirl around the kitchen performing a food prep ballet.

It's like someone hit the Pause button on our dance.

Mom suspends her potato salad stirring, Evie quits dicing the watermelon, and Auntsie halts construction on her veggie tower.

"What? When?" Mom asks.

"In less than forty-eight hours."

Auntsie looks like her head might pop off her shoulders like a bottle rocket. "That's crazy talk. I thought this was settled. What about classes and the job lead from Ricky you told us about? We *talked* about this."

When I got home last night, after we replayed the success of Auntsie's cowbell debut and the gig as the whole, I told them about Ricky calling and offering to hook me up with an actual paying job at Atlantic Trax, where we recorded. I can't believe he went ahead and talked to the owner for me. Ricky is definitely one of the good guys.

I look down at my bare feet, where Reggie has just licked my big toe. I scoop him up.

"It's only for three months."

"Only? You can't expect the job to be there when you get back," Auntsie says.

"No. But college will be. And I'm sure Caleb would take me back. He understands. Sometimes people are more important than jobs."

"Oh really? Well, maybe Malcolm should stay then," Auntsie says.

Bringing Caleb into the conversation stirred old feelings in my aunt. I wish I'd left him out of it.

"I would never ask him to cancel his tour for me. You know why this is so important to him. He was sitting right there when he told you." I point to the chair where Malcolm sat when he came for Sunday dinner. It seems so long ago.

"So, what're you going to do?" I can't tell if Evie's curious or upset.

"I don't know."

Surprisingly, Mom reacts not like her usual Type A self, but like someone who has taken back-to-back yoga and meditation classes.

"Well, I don't want to rush you, hon. But you need to decide. I'm not sure how one begins to pack for a road trip like that. I was going to try to beat the holiday traffic tomorrow, but Evie and I can stick around a little later and help you."

Auntsie looks at Mom, incredulous. "You're okay with this, Gem?"

My, my, my, how times have changed.

Mom looks at me when she answers. "It's Quinn's decision. I trust her."

Auntsie stiffens. "Well, if you're leaving, you need to break it to Reggie. He's gotten quite attached to you."

I kiss the top of Reggie's head and he licks my cheek. "I've gotten attached to him too. I love him. And I'm grateful for the unconditional love he has for me. I hope he'll understand that I'll be back."

I meet Auntsie's eyes. Emotion flickers there for a second, and then she re-hits the play button on party prep.

"Okay then, chop, chop. Let's getting moving. We've got people coming over in an hour. It's time to light the grill."

"Light it up!" Evie cries. It's possible she'll be imitating Ricky for the rest of her life. I hope that night in the studio isn't the most exciting thing that ever happens to her.

People start arriving a little while later. In addition to Caleb, Auntsie has invited our entire block, her coworkers, some people from the shelter, and Kiki and Liam to her annual barbecue. Malcolm's spending the day with his parents, but we agreed to spend tomorrow together. If I don't go on tour, it might be the last time we see each other for a while and he wants to do something special.

The party at Auntsie's house goes on well into the night. The backyard is strung up with paper lanterns, and stereo speakers have been propped in open windows so we can hear Caleb's music mix outside. He assumed the role of DJ shortly after arriving, dressed as an adult for the second time in two days. The only time he leaves Auntsie's side is to put on another record. And Auntsie? She's been walking around with a wineglass in one hand and a grill spatula in the other, Reggie strapped across her torso in one of those baby carriers made for dogs. A pooch pouch, I think she called it. She's soaking in Caleb's attention, and he looks at her so adoringly it's like she's wearing a ball gown and tiara instead of a dog strapped to her chest. Mom sits at the picnic table with Auntsie's coworkers, while Evie, Ashley, and Kate chat up the neighbors' nephews who are here for the holiday.

The chilly easterly breeze carries the promise of cooler autumn nights, prompting Caleb to get the fire pit going while Auntsie breaks out the ingredients for s'mores.

"Hey, so the ever-elusive Andrew remains a mystery. I never did get to meet him last night. I'm beginning to think this friend of yours is imaginary," I tell Liam as I wink at Kiki.

The three of us are reclining in Adirondack chairs around the fire. Bob Marley's "Redemption Song" drifts toward us through the open windows.

Liam scowls. "He never made it there. Something about a camp counselor party."

"Ah, well. Some other time." My mind turns toward the tour. "So, are you all packed?"

"If by packed, you mean thrown two pairs of jeans and five T-shirts into a duffel bag, then yes. I'm ready to go." Liam clicks his tongue and gives me a thumbs-up.

"That's all you're bringing? I notice you never mentioned underwear." I imagine life on the road with four boys will be challenging and somewhat smelly. "You better throw deodorant in too or I'm definitely out."

Kiki laughs and nudges Liam's leg with her flip-flopped foot.

"Hear that? You better smell good for Quinny. She's the only girl you're allowed to smell good for."

"What's the verdict, Q? You do realize it's shit-or-get-off-the-pot time."

"Liam!" Kiki says.

"What? You know what I'm saying. It's go time."

Kiki jumps to my defense. "Don't rush her. Maybe she'd rather stay here with me. You know, September is local summer at the Jersey shore, Quinny. We can have a blast."

My aunt has told me all about local summer—warm September waters, empty beaches. It's what everyone around here lives for.

"Keeks, there will be other local summers. Q may never get another chance to tour with a band. It's a no-brainer."

"It's not that simple," I say.

"Yeah, Liam. Sometimes people need to decide what they're willing to sacrifice for a relationship," Kiki says. "She's got her own life, you know."

Liam reaches for Kiki's hand. "Malcolm would owe Q big time. He knows that."

Kiki leans over and kisses him on the lips. Something tells me these two need to be alone.

I stand. "I'm going to get more sticks for the fire."

Liam keeps his eyes on Kiki when he talks. "I think we're going to take off, Q."

Good. Saves me the "get a room" speech.

We hug over the dying embers.

"I hope I see you at Malcolm's on Tuesday morning, Q. But if not, I'll see you at Keegan's in three months."

"Godspeed," I tell Liam.

Kiki gives me a squeeze. "Night, Quinny. We'll hang out next weekend if you're around."

I watch them leave and sit back down, not bothering to throw another log on the fire as I put up the hood on my sweatshirt and watch the paper lanterns strung up overhead bob. They're rising skyward like giant fireflies bound together, trying to take flight.

FORTY-FOUR

Alone in my room after everyone has left, I'm too wired to sleep, so I unearth my carry-on-sized luggage from the closet and begin to pack. I start with every pair of panties I own, because while I'm fine with recycling jeans and an occasional tee, clean underwear is non-negotiable. I throw in my combat boots and the Virginia Woolf book, which I still haven't finished, then look at the clock. It's after one. I zip the suitcase and leave it on the chair beside my bed, and open my closet, pulling out a sundress. After a quick change, I head to the bathroom to brush my teeth and swipe on some mascara before tiptoeing barefoot down the steps, carrying my flip-flops.

I'm rounding the corner toward the kitchen and the back door when Mom's voice beckons me from the couch.

"Quinn?"

I walk over and sit on the coffee table beside her. Reggie is hunkered down at her feet.

"Tell Malcolm I said 'hello.' I'm glad I got the chance to meet him at your gig. He seems like a good guy."

"He is, Mom. For once."

"You deserve it, baby. I know you thought I was too hard on you about the others, especially that creeper of a teacher, but I wanted more for you. It hurt me to see you pursuing people and things that would hurt you."

"I know that now."

"Have you made your decision?"

"I think I have."

"Text me when you get to Malcolm's."

"I will."

She sits up and gives me a hug, squeezing me tighter than necessary, but I don't mind. I could get used to it.

"You'll call me tomorrow?" she asks.

"Yes. And every day after that. Love you, Mom."

"Love you too. More than you'll ever know. Be safe."

My mind and body are on autopilot as I drive across the bay bridge toward Malcolm's place. When I find myself in front of the garage tapping in the four-digit code, I barely remember getting here. As the garage door slowly rolls open, I see the space has been cleared of all music gear in anticipation of the house sale. I walk to the spot where my borrowed drums once stood and then look toward the kitchen door. It's open.

My heart breaks a little wondering how many nights he left it that way for me.

I walk up the two steps and into the kitchen. The nearly empty house is quiet as I draw closer to the enormous flat screen that glows silently and casts shadows on the family room ceiling. I find Malcolm there, in the exact position I knew he would be in—reclining on the couch, our couch, with headphones on, staring intently at the screen. When I step between him and the TV's glow, he whips off the headphones, stands, and walks toward me. He's shirtless and wearing the gray sweat shorts he usually sleeps in. I notice fresh ink on the inside of his bicep and brush my fingertips along the three words I can't understand.

"It's Latin," he says, reading the quizzical look on my face.

I'm about to ask him what the words mean, but instead he wraps his arms around my waist and we fall into a kiss. The second his lips touch mine, deciphering his tattoo becomes the furthest thing from my mind. I dig my fingers into his bare shoulders as he leads me toward the couch in a slightly awkward waltz while we continue to kiss. Neither of us wants to let go, but I finally pull away, resting my hands on his chest and pushing him down gently, until he's seated on the couch. I remain standing before him, watching the way his pupils have dilated. He runs his fingers along my bare thighs, and in one swift motion, I slip my dress over my head and kick off my flip-flops.

"Cat's Eye," he whispers. "Is this happening?"

I answer his question by removing what's left of what I'm wearing. He wraps his arms around my waist and kisses my stomach, and then, without hesitation, I press his shoulders until he is on his back. I lay my body beside his, knowing that if this is our last night together, this is exactly how I want our story to end.

We move together wordlessly, our bodies alternately in tandem and in sync, responding to each other's movements like a perfectly orchestrated song. The patio doors are open, and I swear I hear music in the wind coming off the bay. It's a tune so personal and familiar that I don't know why it takes me so long to realize that it's coming from inside me.

Afterward, Malcolm cradles me in his arms and I lay my head on his chest, listening as his rapidly beating heart slows to its normal tempo. He plays with my hair and we both fight sleep, neither of us wanting this night to end.

"I love you, Quinn," he says right before I fall asleep.

I lift my head and kiss him.

"I love you too." I lay my head back down, close my eyes, and start to drift away. "Goodnight, Malcolm," I whisper, but what I really mean is "Goodbye."

I'm up before Malcolm the next day, awakened by the

sounds of morning stirring outside. I slip out from under his arm and leave him sleeping, stepping into my sundress and grabbing a throw blanket before walking through the patio doors and down to the dock. The air is chilly and still, the bay like glass. The crickets are fading and the birds' song grows louder. It won't be long before I see the sun.

On the dock's edge, I dangle my feet over the water and wrap the blanket tighter around my shoulders. The water laps gently against the pilings and I keep my eyes on the horizon, which is capped with pale light. When I hear footsteps behind me, I'm not surprised. I knew it wouldn't take him long to find me. We are connected forever, he and I, bound together by the guilt and sorrow that nearly shattered us and the one summer that made us whole. I know I'll never feel this way about anyone ever again, but that's okay. Sometimes that's how it's supposed to be, right? It's like what Malcolm said all those weeks ago when I rescued his drunken ass from the boardwalk: People come together for different reasons at different times. It doesn't mean you're destined to stay together forever. But if you're lucky, you'll leave each other in a better place.

I let the blanket drop from my shoulders and he sits down behind me, wrapping a leg on either side of me. I lay back against him, and he encircles my shoulders with his arms.

I feel his warm breath against my hair. His voice hums inside me when he speaks.

"You aren't coming with me, are you?"

I shake my head and lay my cheek against his bicep, pressing my lips to each inked word.

"A new day," Malcolm says.

Neither of us says another word as we wait for ours to begin.

FORTY-FIVE
(CODA)

It's less than a month until Halloween, and I'm sitting on a barstool at Keegan's reading a book as I wait for the first band to start their sound check.

I've helped Caleb spruce up the place with a mixture of black garland, orange lights, and some well-placed pumpkins and gourds, which I painted black and gray to ensure the club looks edgy, not like a marriage between a seafood restaurant and farmer's market. I even lit some tea light candles along the bar.

"Quinn!" Caleb calls to me from the stage. "These guys are ready!"

I close my book and keep it with me as I walk toward the board. Virginia Woolf might be the death of me, but I refuse to give up on *To the Lighthouse* and Auntsie's reading list, even though I started college classes this week and my life just got a lot busier. There's homework, Reggie duty, my jobs here and at Atlantic Trax, and Sundays at the shelter, where Auntsie and I continue to do God's work. I'm not complaining. I need to keep busy. It makes me forget who's missing.

"Hey, guys," I say to the band. "Let's hear some guitar first."

A dude in skinny jeans and a gray tee strums a few chords, and I make some minor adjustments.

"How's that?" I ask.

He strums some more and frowns. "Can you turn me up some more?"

Diva, I hear Liam say. It's only been a few weeks, but I miss that old douchebag. Of course, I miss Malcolm more. We agreed not to talk or text while he's on tour. It would be too hard. We're still tethered together, but the threads of that connection are stretching and fraying with every mile. I'm both welcoming and dreading the day when I stop thinking about where I am now in relation to the distance between us.

I've been good about avoiding the band's social media feeds. It helps that I'd already abandoned all my accounts after the unfortunate tree branch incident, but I do welcome my almost daily updates from Kiki and Liam. How else would I know that, as expected, Malcolm's label made him an offer? They want to sign him as a solo act to record a full-length album with Ricky at his

Nashville studio. Any future tours will be with a backing band of the label's choosing, not Malcolm's, which works out for a variety of reasons. Specifically, Liam's determined to start Rutgers in January, and Travis is turning out to be a bit of an asshole.

Don't worry though, Q. Malcolm's got it under control and I've got his back, Liam texted me.

I knew Liam would.

I signal to the drummer to start sound check, and he pounds the kick drum a few times.

"Good. Now give me some hi-hat." I'm about to have him move on to the snare drum when someone taps me on the shoulder.

"Need any help?" asks a male voice behind me.

I turn to see a guy in a green wool beanie that clashes with his auburn hair. He has eyes shaped like crescent moons and a slight gap between his front teeth that make his smile imperfectly perfect. He looks familiar, but I don't know why.

"Quinn?" he asks.

"Yeeeah," I say slowly.

He offers me his hand, and I take it, surprised by how it warms me with a familiarity that makes me want to hang on a little longer.

"Andrew Clark. I wasn't sure if it was you. Liam said you wore...glasses."

I laugh. "He said ugly glasses, didn't he?" I keep forgetting to tell him I've gone back to contacts. I haven't worked on improving my wardrobe though.

"You know him well," Andrew says.

"And I feel like I know you."

"Same here. Glad I finally got to meet the infamous Q."

It's nice to hear my nickname again.

Andrew points to my book.

"Hey, *To the Lighthouse*! I did my senior thesis on Virginia Woolf. I'm practically an expert on that book."

"Really?" I say, mulling over the possibilities.

"So, do you need any help?" he asks again, nodding toward the board.

"With sound? No. Woolf? Maybe."

He laughs. "Cool tat, by the way."

My hand moves reflexively to my wrist. Auntsie's favorite artist had a cancellation and was able to squeeze me in. A Celtic knotwork design now covers my scar.

"Does it mean anything?" Andrew asks.

"Forgiveness," I say.

I have no idea if that's true, but that's what it means to me.

"Cool." He points over his shoulder. "Well, I'll be over by the bar if you need me."

I pat my book. "Maybe we can talk about this later?"

"Sure. I'm not going anywhere. In fact, I was hoping Caleb would give me my old job back. I may be around for a while."

My heart tugs skyward when he says that, like the string of paper lanterns straining in the wind. I embrace the sensation and turn to face the band.

"Play me a song," I tell them. The drummer clacks his sticks to count them in…one, two, three, four…and when the music starts, all at once I feel my heart break free.

AUTHOR'S NOTE

Every day, ninety-one Americans die from opioid overdoses, according to the Centers for Disease Control and Prevention.

Since 2000, opioid overdoses have killed more than three hundred thousand Americans, and the epidemic has touched nearly every community in the United States. Ocean County, New Jersey, where *August and Everything After* takes place, has been hit particularly hard by the opioid addiction crisis.

Too often, opioid addiction begins with the misuse of prescription pain medications like morphine, oxycodone, or an acetaminophen like Vicodin. A 2014 National Survey on Drug Use and Health (NSDUH) showed that fifteen million people in the United States misused or abused prescription drugs that year.

The opioid addiction epidemic continues to be a national problem, but help is available.

If you or someone you know is battling an addiction to prescription pain medication, heroin, or any other opioid or controlled substance, here are a few of the many resources.

- The **Substance Abuse and Mental Health Services Administration** (SAMHSA) has a twenty-four-hour, year-round helpline, which provides referrals to local treatment facilities, support groups, and community-based organizations.

  Call 1-800-662-HELP (4357) or visit samhsa.gov or samhsa.gov/sites/default/files/ssadirectory.pdf for a direct link to state-funded treatment facilities.

- The **National Council on Alcoholism and Drug Dependence** (NCADD) provides information about addiction and treatment and operates a twenty-four-hour Hope Line at 1-800-622-2255, or you can visit ncadd.org.

- **DrugAbuse.com** provides information on addiction and rehabilitation and connects people with treatment facilities by state. Visit the website or call the twenty-four-hour hotline at 1-877-629-0265.

- The **Partnership for Drug-Free Kids** helps families struggling with a child's addiction. Reach them at 1-855-DRUGFREE (1-855-378-4373) or visit drugfree.org.
- **Narcotics Anonymous** offers information about support and helps addicts find local meetings. Visit na.org.
- The **Suicide Prevention Hotline** at 1-800-273-TALK (8255) operates twenty-four hours a day and helps put callers in touch with the nearest local crisis centers. Visit suicidepreventionlifeline.org.

ACKNOWLEDGMENTS

"Who run the world? Girls." I know it's true in my corner of the globe, where books for teens and kids thrive thanks to many talented, dedicated women. As further evidence that Beyoncé got it right, I present the following list of ladies who contributed to this book in ways both big and small:

Lauren Bjorkman, Patty Blount, Julia Bognar, Kerry Millerchip Bucci, Adriana Calderon, Jody Casella, Bethany Crandell, Margie Gelbwasser, Theresa Festa Giles, Theresa Berano Goldberg, Kristen Hart Haddock, Jackie Hong, Noelle Kocot-Tomblin, Lori Mallari Lynch, Jen Mann, Becky Osowski, Lisa Ryden Paccio, Tija Pavlovic, Jen Post, Rebecca Post, Lisa Reiss, Kim Sabatini, and Diana Rose Verbeck. Thank you for caring enough to make my work better!

Thank you to Kerry Sparks and Annette Pollert-Morgan for seeing something worthwhile in my early writing and sticking with me. Your continued support means everything. Three is the magic number! Thank you to Dominique Raccah, Todd Stocke, Cassie Gutman, Sarah Kasman, Nicole Hower, Danielle McNaughton, Stephany Daniel, and the entire amazing Sourcebooks team.

To my ridiculously supportive family and friends, especially Mom and Dad, Melissa and Anthony Collucci, and Mom D. and Dad D. Your love and encouragement make anything possible.

To my husband, Mike, a talented bass player who I interviewed more than two decades ago when he was a guy in a band and I was a minor rock journalist. Without him, my musical knowledge would be limited to "Soft Sounds of the '70s." (Just one of the many ways my life became infinitely better when I walked into the Budapest Cocktail Lounge, an old-man bar turned indie rock club.) To our daughter, who inspires me every day with the thoughtfulness, intelligence, tenacity, and heart she brings to everything she does. It's no wonder Ravenclaw is the house for you. I love you both so much. You are my heart.

Thank you to YA Outside the Lines, the East Brunswick Public Library Adult Writers' Group, and my favorite librarians, Melissa Hozik and Jessica Schneider, for giving me a forum for my books.

Thank you to the Original Ben Franklin 5 & 10 Store in

Lavallette, New Jersey, and the Shore and More General Store in Seaside Park, New Jersey, for allowing my books to take up counter space.

Thank you to the many talented bands and musicians who create with their music the kind of connections that bring people together and make the world seem less scary and lonely.

Finally, to our dear friend Eric "Ricky" Kvortek, a talented musician and recording engineer who lost his brave fight with brain cancer in 2017. My knowledge of the recording process came from Eric, who is most certainly hard at work auto-tuning the angels. Rock on, my friend. You are loved and missed.

ABOUT THE AUTHOR

Jennifer Salvato Doktorski is the author of three other YA novels, *How My Summer Went Up in Flames*, *Famous Last Words*, and *The Summer After You and Me*, a YALSA Teens' Top Ten nominee. She lives with her family in New Jersey, spending her summers "down the shore," where everything's always all right. You can find out more about her at jendoktorski.com.

Are you
FIRED UP about YA?

Don't Miss the HOT New YA Newsletter
from Sourcebooks Fire

FIREreads

§ #GetBookLit

FEATURING:

Author interviews
Galley giveaways
Exclusive early content
What's new each month
...and more!

Visit books.sourcebooks.com/firereads-ya to sign up!

Follow the FIREreads team and share your
burning love for YA with #GetBookLit:

 @sourcebooksfire   sourcebooksfire

 SourcebooksFire   firereads.tumblr.com

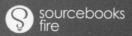